R/evolution

R/evolution

A Mosaic Novel, Book One

Tenea D. Johnson

counterpoise (koun´tər poiz´), *n., v.:* both a balancing force
and the equilibrium it creates—books and compositions, stories to
music, timeless records.

"The Taken," first published in *Whispers in the Night: Dark Dreams III*, edited by Brandon Massey, Dafina, 2007.

counterpoise
Box 341
St. Petersburg, Fl 33731

CONTENTS

How the Carters Got Their Name

A lot of Black folks are walking around with their owner's last name. Or rather their ancestor's owner. Others are a little luckier. They're Johnson from Son of John. Baker 'cause that's what they did. Cobbler from the skill it took to earn that name. Ezekiel was one of these last. Sometimes he wished he were a son of John, though – 'cause the Carters had earned their name in death, and revolution.

His grandmother only told Ezekiel the story once. He had just finished weeding their garden and stood in the kitchen, gulping down sweet iced tea. Outside it had been hot like it only got in the moist river valley of Kentucky: hot enough to take notice, but not to impose too much on the beautiful day. Grandma Maddie called him into the living room. She sat in her overstuffed armchair, watching one of the reparations protests with the sound turned off. A throng of brown faces filled the small screen, mouthing the same words. Their expressions said more than the placards they held, articulated their position better than a thousand raised fists. Grandma Maddie looked up from the scene and told Ezekiel to sit so she could tend to the rose bush scratches riddled down his arms. He settled at the foot of her chair, his shoulder resting against her knee. With both of Ezekiel's parents long ago passed away – his mother, into the grave, and his father, into the night – Ezekiel and Grandma Maddie

The chair bounced off and slammed into the corner of the wall. It had left a small crack and scratch in the plexi where it made contact.

"Back away." The deep booming voice belonged to the huge guy who'd been anchoring the last row of seats. At his full height he must have been 6'6" and twice Ezekiel's weight. He didn't acknowledge Professor Szlasa as he picked up the chair and approached the window. He hit it full force; the jolt of the impact sent the chair back at him and he turned his hip and shoulder just in time to avoid knocking himself in the head. On his next shot, he held the chair at shoulder-level like he was taking a pitch.

"What's the time?" he called out.

"3:12!" someone yelled back.

Professor Szlasa tried to take charge of the situation.

"Stop that! That is school property!" he said feebly. "Everyone just calm down. I'll contact administration."

This seemed to pacify a few students in the middle of the room, who had been watching the scene, askance. They sat down in the nearest chairs, whispering to each other as they watched the guys at the window, pounding away at the plexi. Ezekiel looked over at Addie as Professor Szlasa had called her. He guessed she wasn't new after all. She walked away from the windows to the exit. When she reached it, she pushed her face as close as she could into the small window embedded in the metal door, peering out into the hallway. She looked down both directions.

Ezekiel approached her.

"That's probably not plexi," he said.

She turned around and sized him up at a glance.

"No, probably not. Good eye." She looked around the room, ostensibly for something to bust it with.

"I overlooked that. Panic, you know," she said. "I should see if anyone has anything." She started toward the rest of the students. "If we can get through maybe we can reach the keypad on the other side."

"Maybe we're stuck inside for a reason," Ezekiel responded.

Addie turned back to Ezekiel.

"Yeah, but I don't particularly want to find out what that reason is. Do you–" she paused and looked at him expectantly.

"Ezekiel," he responded.

"Do you, Ezekiel?"

"No," Ezekiel said.

"I got through!" the lanky brown-haired boy stared at his handheld. "I got through to the net. It's everywhere."

Questions filled the room, loudest among them, 'What's everywhere?'

"People locked in schools. Looks like some dorms and apartment buildings too," he responded.

"What do they know?" someone called out.

"Hold on." He brought the handheld closer to his face and began to read aloud.

"Reports are pouring in that there may be a terroristic threat underway . . ." he read.

The small group seated in the middle of the room exclaimed: "Oh my god! Oh my God!"

"Is there anything specific?" Addie asked.

The boy shot her a dirty look and appeared to skim ahead, running his finger across the small screen.

He shook his head as he mouthed the words.

"No," he looked up slowly still shaking his head. "No. They're just saying what's happening as it happens."

Ezekiel spoke up above the clamour.

"We need something, strong and long. Small enough to fit through the window," he said, pointing at the door. "Does anyone have–"

"I know circuitry," Addie said. "Maybe we can short the lock out and get out that way."

"What if the danger is outside?" someone said from the back.

"That doesn't make any sense," another student responded. Ezekiel looked around the room for Professor Szlasa. The professor sat at one of the desks, listening as he dialed on his handheld.

Ezekiel looked around the room for a suitable tool. He picked up one of the desks and with Addie's help worked to separate the metal leg from the plastic. The first two bolts busted cleanly with a few kicks. Still, the leg remained attached to the frame.

"Let's just bend the rest of the chair out of the way." Addie said.

"I've got it. Just get what you need for the circuits," he responded. Ezekiel paid little attention to everyone else in the room. He kicked at the desk leg until it jutted out from the twisted frame. The argument continued.

"There's no way of knowing if it's inside our outside."

"There is. He said people are locked in everywhere. Everywhere else can't be dangerous."

"Why not? It was fine 10 minutes ago!"

Time. Ezekiel stopped and looked down at his handheld. The room went temporarily silent; when he glanced up he saw that the combatants looked at their handhelds as well.

1:00. He picked the chair up and with all of his strength bashed the leg into the small window in the door. The glass fractured. With the next blow the leg shattered through. He caught the chicken wire inside the window around the leg and pulled it out. Before he could ask, Addie was there at his elbow. She held a small eyeglass screwdriver. Ezekiel stepped out of the way to give her

for slavery, none was more feared than New Dawn. They didn't want educational vouchers or free medical care like the other groups, they wanted everything – land redistribution, financial compensation, and stock in every conglom that had benefited from slavery. And even by 2024, that was all the conglomerations. Worse, New Dawn didn't believe in legislation or picketing or economic sanctions. They believed in results. The one and only press statement New Dawn ever issued said just that: "We believe in results." Those words perplexed people outside of political circles. It worried her father's camp. Like Kristen, they knew what it took to get results.

A man in a black mask sat on a low stool outside of Kristen's cage. He'd been staring at Margaret Eastland for the last few hours, the hours she'd spent screaming. Now he looked in Kristen's direction. He turned his eyes slowly, as if measuring each inch between them. Kristen's lip quivered, shivers turned to jolts as he turned his full attention on her. Like the dozen other men outside the cages, he was dressed in all black, a mesh mask obscuring his features. It was hard to tell his height, but he seemed big holding a long stun stick. He tapped it on the floor every few minutes, sending blue sparks dancing along the concrete. Kristen tried to look him in the eye, but the mask stopped her. It had an opalescent sheen, making it seem to float in front of his face. The Mask looked her up and down, stopping at her stomach, her breasts, her bent shoulders and sweaty face. The longer he looked, the more her throat tightened, the harder it became to breathe. She tried to distract herself, craning her neck to look into the men's cage, but her skin prickled with the weight of his stare. Kristen turned back, looked down at the scratches on her hands, the dirt under her fingernails. After thirty minutes, she began to understand why Eastland screamed.

Somewhere inside the building a door slammed. Kristen jumped, jabbing her elbow into one of the bars. The Mask laughed at her, then fell silent, staring up at the landing behind the cages. For a moment, she could see the man beneath the mask, the reverence that smoothed out the tight lines around his mouth. She followed his gaze.

Phillip Tailor, New Dawn's leader, wore no mask; instead he donned a smile. Like the others, he wore black fatigues. In place of the mask, a pair of opaque glasses covered his eyes. A tall man, he towered over the cages and Kristen felt a spell of vertigo. Tailor nodded acknowledgment at the man guarding Kristen's cage. Leaning gracefully over the railing, he surveyed the busy warehouse floor. Another Mask, much smaller than Tailor, walked up to him. The Mask said something in that gibberish language and, with another nod, Tailor was gone.

Abruptly, Eastland stopped screaming. The Mask returned to his original posture, leaving a trail of blue sparks as he slowly dragged the stun stick back to his side. Margaret Eastland slumped against the bars, fingers twitching the last of the voltage from her system. The blonde girl scurried farther away from the prone body, pinning Kristen into the corner. Kristen was grateful for the sweat pressed into her skin, grateful for someone to hold onto, and come between her and the apparition who scrutinized her, sparking blue intention across the floor.

Their captors were yelling more. Still holding the blonde girl, Kristen tried to follow one set of gibberish from man to man. The tone suggested commands, but she couldn't be sure. She looked towards the sound of a bodega gate coming down. This gate was much bigger and going up. The whole wall behind the barracoons recessed into its upper reaches and let dawn in. She smelled saltwater, heard distant traffic, and hoped for a moment. Maybe New Dawn had gotten their ransom. Maybe her father had arrived. Maybe someone would see them and send agents. Maybe, maybe.

Her brain stuttered at the sight of the gangplank. It could hardly take in the ship and open water beyond it. She opened her mouth to scream. Hours of sitting hadn't slowed the Mask. He lunged with precision, knocking over his stool. The stun stick passed through the barracoons bars and touched Kristen's shoulder. Still clutching each other, she and the blonde girl shared the strong current.

Conscious, but unable to move, Kristen watched as her hand slipped from the tangle of blonde hair receding from her grasp. After New Dawn dragged the younger girl out, they pulled at Kristen's ankles. She felt the silk, then her skin, tear against the rough floor. When her head fell from the cage's lip and onto the concrete, she whimpered.

The Mask hovered close to her face, squinting at her. He reached down and pinched her ear. Hard. Her hand jumped. He grunted low in his throat, snatched her up by her armpits so that they were face to face. She heard him exchange a few words with someone. Another set of hands held her from behind, her head resting against a broad chest. Her gaze followed the other women being dragged out of the door and into the half-light – then out of her field of vision.

The man behind the mask peeled it up from the bottom, stopped just above his lips. A translation patch stuck to the mesh's underside. Now the gibberish made sense.

"Say goodbye to home," he said, his voice clear and deep without the conversion.

The hands behind her covered her mouth and lifted her away from the barracoon, towards the ship.

•

She was trying to remember the diagrams. All her life, she'd flipped past the Black History Month specials, those horrible images somebody should have forgotten by now. But now she wished she could remember. Then at least she would have some idea what the hold looked like. Maybe then she'd know where the blonde girl was and where they'd put the men. She could feel flesh, but the heat made it difficult to tell which was hers. The Masks hadn't been back down since they'd chained the captives to each other, and then the ship. And she'd been near unconsciousness then.

Someone coughed. Was that a man's cough or a woman's? Did it matter? Someone was awake. She tried to use her voice. When she heard it, it sounded like she'd been up for days, high on too much Mystique.

"Bridget?" she pleaded into the dark. "Margaret?"

"Matthew." The voice came from beneath her. "Matt Holleran. From Georgia."

Kristen saw a flash of a gangly red-headed boy with green eyes beaming out from an 'Equality is Now!' poster. Senator Holleran and his family had posed for the short-lived campaign that was supposed to help end the call for reparations. She thought back to the faces in the men's cage. There. The one with the dark red beard. Broad-chested, head bent beneath the cage's low ceiling. Matthew Holleran.

"Blake Denning," a voice below her.

"Harry Anderson," and another.

"Preston Caleb," this one from above.

"Bridget Hardy," the skin on her left.

A high-pitched whisper from above, "Margaret Eastland."

"Chuck Lassiter," the skin on her right.

"Drew Ellison."

•

Captain Tailor watched the infrared images calling out their names. He tapped the screen, then turned down the volume. *Should feed them soon. No, just water,* he corrected himself. He'd been battling how many inaccuracies to allow, trying to find the balance between highlighting their advantages and introducing them to the Middle Passage's suffering, so that they could in turn introduce the White world. Though he and his crew were perpetrating one of the most ambitious experiments in the Rep War campaign, he had to maintain parameters. Already, he worried about the Examples' advantages: a shared language, a smaller group, the faster voyage, and of course, all the moral prerogatives: no rape, no dying, limited physical abuse. But he aimed to get the majority into their heads and hopefully their hearts through the body. Identity politics infused with psychological warfare. He knew the formula would get results. He had to remain vigilant if they were to be the right results.

Shireen walked into the surveillance room, still talking on her handheld.

"What's the final count on that?" she sighed, thanked the person on the other line and hung up. She walked towards Tailor, slipping the handheld into her bulky jacket.

"Fifteen dead at the Baltimore demonstration though they're only reporting them as injuries. Over 300 arrests."

"What about Tuscaloosa and DC?" he asked.

She sat down in the chair next to Captain Tailor.

"The Representatives in Tuscaloosa never stopped walking, just got in their transports and bolted. And the PFC postponed the March in DC." She pulled the rolled-up mesh fabric down to her ears. "It's cold in here."

"Again." He answered to both statements. "How many postponements does that make?"

"Three. This time something about one of the organizer's connections to the Court of International Trade muddying the waters."

He laughed. "Once again, nonviolent proves itself nonviable."

Shireen fell silent. They'd always disagreed on this point. He knew that she believed a happy medium existed between the extremes; that she'd signed up for this project to protect the Examples, though Monitor was her official title, and, on the ship, First Mate. That title must have rankled her feminist leanings. But that's exactly why Tailor needed her: Shireen didn't say 'yes' unless she meant it.

Tailor stood and walked over to the heart and blood pressure monitors that made up the center wall. He tore off hard copies of the latest readings and filed them away, made sure the digifiles were simultaneously saving and transmitting to the processors stateside.

It felt good to stand; he'd been at the monitors for nearly two hours, making notes for the first draft of his press statement. He stretched his arms toward the ceiling, looked out the window at the crew taking in the fresh night air. Latrell shared a cigarette with TwoTone. Their light jackets flapped in the breeze, as the smoke swirled around the bill of TwoTone's ever-present cap. Good men, those. They knew enough not to ask questions. He wouldn't have to worry about them; they would do the job and take the freedom offered in Ghana, leave all the restrictions on felons behind and live as full men again. His attention to the details was just as much for this New Dawn crew as for the nine below. The voyage would change them just as profoundly.

He turned back to Shireen who sat, jaw tensed, looking at the surveillance monitors.

"Should we feed them now?"

"Yes," she answered. "I'll go with TwoTone."

"I'll go with you two," Tailor answered. He retrieved a mask from the top of the monitor banks.

Shireen looked at him quizzically.

"Research," he answered to the unspoken question.

Captain Tailor and Shireen collected the stocky man outside. All three pulled their masks down, opalescence shimmering in the moonlight, as they walked.

The hold stank. Even with the masks' air filters, a level of the stench still entered Tailor's nose – a sharp unpleasantness that reached past technology to give him the impression of feces, urine, and vomit. It smelled like the Rep War: everything let go after being pent up too long. Yes, he knew that smell.

Walking past the containers of food and medicines New Dawn would bring onto the shores of West Africa, they reached the back corner where the nine lay, three by three, in a space designed for two industrial sinks. Shireen added powdered protein to the cornmeal mush and handed it to TwoTone who did the water and food detail. Captain Tailor stood nearby, taking notes on a legal pad. He stepped closer and hovered near the middle tier. Shireen climbed atop the structure and searched for an ankle to spray with the antibiotic salve. Tailor heard her sigh; she turned and looked at him, her expression unreadable. She told TwoTone to give everyone extra water. Shireen's words came out in Icelandic. With the trans link in his ear TwoTone understood well enough. After the training, time in the warehouse setting things up and the sea, they could both probably speak the strange language without the aid of trans patches. At first, Shireen had questioned Tailor about his 'odd choice', but now he was sure she understood: who could understand Icelandic? Most people couldn't even recognize it.

•

Kristen dreamt of the sky. Its light gray tones bobbed by, the sun still hidden in dawn's hues: not the sunset sky of her trip to Bali, or the bright blue receding and advancing of her childhood swing, not even the rare red sunrise on the Hudson after a long night of cocktails and conversation. She dreamt of the last sky she saw, bobbing above, as her head bumped on the slats of the pier.

Up on deck, the sky was clearer than Kristen had dreamed it. She kept her eyes on it as she stumbled up and down the small deck. She didn't want to look at the men, the men without their masks. They barked commands in that strange language, though their waving hands made their meaning clear enough. *Here. Go Here. Faster. Faster. Stop. Get Back. Right Now. Do It Again.*

She didn't want to see the others from the hold either. If they could just not look at each other, one day they might be able to see one another without the memory. Kristen doubted that 'one day' would ever come. Apparently, New Dawn didn't care if she and the others saw their faces. So the men would probably kill them out here on the open sea. They believed in results.

When they had to go back to the hold, Kristen missed the light.

•

If left in its grasp too long, the dark crawls over you and molds you into something unrecognizable. Already Kristen's back had changed shape. Fluid filled her lungs. Her skin had become a separate animal that she tried to fight off. She'd been in the dark for five days.

That night the crew came down to choose their bedwarmers. Tailor picked Kristen.

When the two men who'd brought her up took off the blindfold, Tailor was already seated at a small table, a pitcher of amber-colored liquid at his elbow. The room was small. No more than a cot bolted to the floor, and the table. Tailor took the tail of the chain around her wrists from one of the crewmen and bid them good night. As soon as they were gone, he pulled the chain roughly, causing her to stumble closer to the cot. Wrapping the chain around the cot leg, he produced a small lock that he secured to the couplings, and chained her legs to the bottom of the cot.

Tailor, winded, pulled up a chair and posed a question.

"Imagine no one had tended to your brand. How do you think it would look now? How much pain would you be in?"

Kristen didn't answer. Could hardly breathe. Tailor inclined his head slightly and continued.

"Imagine that there were 190 of you instead of nine. What do you think it would smell like? How many would be dying?"

Silence.

"Imagine that you'd had to walk the forty miles between where we captured you and the warehouse. How close to death would you have been in your high heels and silk pajamas?"

Rage moved through her. She bucked in the chains, spraining her wrist, bruising her ankles. She called him every name she could think of. Names she didn't know that she knew. She screamed her throat raw and then lay glaring at him, breath shooting out in short bursts.

Tailor looked at her, smiling a little. Then asked another question.

He went on like that until the sun came up. Just before he called the crewmen to lead her back into the hold he said:

"Now imagine that I had raped you."

The well of tears that had threatened to spill all night, came brimming over Kristen's lids. She leaned against the doorframe, head bowed, trying to hide her face from him.

"Next time," he said looking at her intently, "if you do what I want, you can have some of the peach juice. It's your favorite, no?"

•

On the way back to the hold, the crewmen walked a full foot in front of Kristen. They held her chain away from their bodies and looked down at the floor or out at sea. At the entrance, they waited for Kristen to walk through, careful not to touch her.

She was the last one to be brought back to the hold. Eight shadows filled the bank between the ceiling and floor. They hardly moved, didn't speak though she could hear one of the men on the top row whimpering. One crewman waited at the entrance, while the other dragged the chain across the planks and locked Kristen back in place. The two left silently, footfalls heavy and slow.

The wood beneath Kristen creaked in time to the waves, but there were no human sounds, not from the crew above or the ones down below. It was as if a spell had been cast over everyone on the ship and now each person lie quietly trying to remember how they'd become so afflicted. Kristen supposed this because she, herself, could think of nothing else.

It was enough that her mind was working again. In the last few days, it had abandoned her for long stretches of time, capable of nothing more than the automatic functions of pumping her heart and breathing. Kristen would wait, ambivalent about the return of her awareness. Gradually, it let her hear the sound of scurrying after a long stretch of silence. When she could feel the cold moisture pooled under her buttocks, she knew it had returned. For better or for worse.

Later, she heard the hold door open. Someone above her keened a quick note of terror. She watched as a shaft of light knifed through the dark, growing larger and brighter. Chains knocked against wood as the captives shifted, trying to curl away.

The door closed. When Kristen's eyes adjusted, four of the crewmen stood at her feet. They'd already unlocked the men on the bottom row; now they worked on her manacles.

Up on deck, the captives huddled near each other. The remnants of their clothes hung at odd angles. All the silk that had once covered Kristen's back was worn away leaving only deep scratches on her reddened skin. She looked better than most of the other women. The crew kept their distance. No one shouted for dancing or prodded them with the short end of a stun stick. A half a dozen crewmen stood against the railing, staring out into the sea. Others dragged fire hoses into the hold to blast out its offal. These were the same men who had hauled the women and two of the men away last night, their shouts louder than the captives' pleas; today, they looked stooped, a little less full.

•

"Bedwarmers, Phillip!" Shireen stood in the middle of the monitor room, arms across her chest, glaring at Captain Tailor.

"It's good to finally hear you call me by my first name, Shireen."

She clenched her teeth until a solid square of tread emerged from the corners of her jaw.

"You watched the monitors all night. Did anything happen?" he asked.

"Hell yes, something happened – you went too far."

"Too far?" Tailor flared with his own anger now; his voice went quiet and steady. "This is <u>nothing</u>! A few questions and an uncomfortable night at the foot of someone's bed. Why Latrell even gave up his bed! Too far? They're not children. They're not dying. This is just a taste of suffering. A taste! They get to go free at the end, Shireen. Their children will be free. Their minds will be free. They won't work a single day. Mark my words: no one will ever deny them their due. Not far enough perhaps, but not *nearly* too far."

•

Kristen heard Tailor's voice and flinched, jerked her head towards the railing. Two of the male captives stared at her. When Kristen saw how the men looked at her, she knew she had become part of their nightmare. And they would never remember her any other way.

•

Tailor sent for her. He shackled her to the table, hands pulled down into her lap by a chain looped under the seat, through the back of the chair, and around her waist. Kristen barely resisted. Fatigue had most of her; the rest stared at the camera and tripod pointed at the small cot in the corner of the room. Tailor pushed her up to the table and placed the pitcher of peach juice below her chin. Kristen's nose worked independently of the rest of her, pulling deep breaths of peach into her mouth and chest. Captain Tailor sat down opposite her. He crossed his legs loosely at the ankle.

She eyed the video camera over his shoulder, a hot knot of foreboding forming in her stomach. She wanted to believe the camera had been there the last time but knew it had not. Tailor's last words to her echoed in her memory. Between them, her pain, abject hunger, and the cold gusting around the edge of the door, it was all she could do to stay conscious – never mind sane.

"Kristen–" Captain Tailor looked directly at her, his tone even.

For twenty-two years, Kristen, Senator Burke's daughter, answered when someone called her name. The new Kristen, woman snatched from her native soil, cried when she heard her name for the first time. She made no sound, only shook with her pain. Every other heartbeat she gasped for breath. Her hands hung loosely in her lap, head dropped straight down into her chest.

Captain Tailor reached behind him to turn the camera around. And started his questioning.

Kristen broke before the agents came, even before they'd reached the Tropic of Cancer. She told Tailor all the answers to his questions. All the ways her passage, differed, bettered. Listed all the things she didn't go through, mentioned the medical care she'd received. Learned his brutal lesson. Tailor had to reload the camera she talked so much. In between answers, she guzzled from the goblet of amber-colored liquid. The juice tasted sweet, better than Kristen remembered.

In the end, Tailor threw away his own draft and broadcast Kristen Burke, dirty, ragged, and grateful as his statement.

The Measure of a Man

Bennett came from a long line of soldiers, and only
soldiers. There were no airmen or women, sailors, or
Marines. The Army was his family's college, a ticket out
of Small Town, Virginia that led to a life beyond parking
lot parties and pumping gas. The tailor, crouched now at
Bennett's instep with a tape measure, knew this because
he had heard it from the Bennetts before. The tailor had
no doubt that Bennett had learned to fire a gun before he
could multiply. It had been the same with Bennett's
father and great uncle. They took it as a point of pride,
bragging to him as he measured their inseams, pinned
their cuffs in place. They had looked down on him as
they told their stories, rolling their shoulders and finally
shaking their heads as if they had been foolish to try and
share such matters with him. Often they took a pedantic
tone as they explained that they didn't intend their
greatness, it was just inevitable. The irritating
predictability of it all was part of the tradition – as far as
the tailor was concerned.

It had begun with the shop's original owner during
the Vietnam War. The first Bennett had strode in and
asked to have a suit made, his funeral suit he said. The
previous owner told the tailor that that Bennett had said
something about Buddhist monks taking a shovelful of
dirt from their own graves each day, as well as a vague
inaccuracy about Sioux warriors. That Bennett had seen a
special on TV that explained these traditions, and it had

inspired him to come into the shop to request the double-breasted, shawl lapel jacket he'd always dreamed of – whether in preparation or motivation, the original owner had not been sure.

And so it had been with each war: a new suit, a new Bennett. Some of the suits were eventually worn at homecoming parties; others were later cut straight down the back in preparation for the grave. Now the tailor and the latest Bennett found themselves here enacting the tedious drama all over again.

But this boy was not a soldier. As he worked, the tailor learned that this Bennett wouldn't be off to boot camp soon or shipping out to some dusty foreign outpost in two weeks. He told the tailor that he was already on the frontlines – of the 'Rep War' – hunting down 'naturalized illegals' as he called them and by his own description he should have been a sergeant. Upon hearing this, the tailor pushed a pin through the thin cloth and into the boy's skin. Bennett jumped and let out a tight little yell. The tailor smiled imperceptibly.

The tailor was as hungry as anyone else in the neighborhood and so would take the boy's money, but did not owe him any comfort or respect. He leaned over and turned on some music. Thankfully he could now hardly hear Bennett's protests. Sudden yelling on the street, however, broke through his curtain of calm. But until a chunk of rock flew through the front window, the tailor ignored that too.

The explosion of glass and noise shut the boy up. He hopped down from the small platform and hurried to the entrance. From where the tailor now stood he saw a mob, comprised of men he was sure had families but apparently no sense, as it closed in on a lone man. And to his danger these days so soon after the kidnappings, it was a Black man. He ran down the street, sweat pouring down his brow, as his gaze searched frantically for some means of escape.

"Yeah!!" Bennett yelled as he hopped up on the window seat with his palms up near his chest, clearly intending to tackle the man as he passed.

The tailor, who until now had stayed at the back of the shop, stepped forward. From the nearest drawer, he pulled the .38 his daughter had insisted he keep in the shop; the comforting weight of his heavy shears hit his thigh as he walked to the window and, just in time, pushed Bennett aside. The Black man, wearing Glen plaid shorts the tailor noticed, jumped over the threshold of the broken window and landed in the middle of the shop.

The tailor pointed to the phone and waited for the mob to arrive.

He had never shot anyone and had not intended to start doing so today, but standing at the broken window where the wind could now caress his face, the tailor thought how quickly things could change. Behind him the music softly played.

RPMs

Sirens, long and loud, penetrated the darkness. Even with his eyes closed, Ezekiel could not escape their urgency, could not find a few moments rest and with a small grunt he gave up trying. He took a last look at the dim stars above him and slowly walked back to the emergency room. Officially, Grey Corporation called the room a receiving center, as they did for all their clinics, but tonight the bright, formerly pristine space was exactly what they claimed it not to be.

Stretchers of injured activists and North Birmingham residents lined the walls. Apparently a group of environmental protestors had clashed with the industrial landfill's security detail, bringing police and residents into the fray as the violence spread throughout the neighborhood of North Birmingham. Now, moans of pain from the waiting area floated past the nurses' station where still more people waited. One stretcher stood away from the others. Small speckles of blood gathered on the sheet covering someone who had not made it to the clinic in time. An attendant rushed past Ezekiel and pushed the body around the corner, out of sight. Watching the departure, Ezekiel wondered if they even had a morgue on the premises.

Grey Corp clinics were not full-service hospitals, technically not hospitals at all. They were designed to provide maintenance care for their participants and stabilize those with life-threatening injuries until they could be transferred to a private hospital, home, or to the county morgue. Usually, Grey Corp didn't get anyone who had private insurance and access to hospitals – not on this side of the campus anyway. Ezekiel longed to be back on the other side of the campus, in the enhancement center lab where during his internship he spent ten hours of each day processing the genetic samples collected here at the clinic. Those samples were the price of admission. Sitting in the quiet, isolated lab he had thought the arrangement must have been a good thing for the participants. Without Grey Corp they, like his Grandma Maddie and millions of other Americans, would have no health care at all. More than once, he'd wondered if the people here on the clinic side cared that their DNA and the knowledge Grey Corp gained from it would help the private customers seated comfortably in the enhancement center's reception lounge.

No one was there now. Only he, Addie, and a few other interns had been called in to start their clinic rotation early and help with the fallout of the protest at the North Birmingham landfill. The clinic held the people who had agreed to provide samples in exchange for treatment. No doubt, there were some regular participants among them; the risks and realities of living next door to the industrial landfill were well known. Ezekiel wondered how many more potential patients were in that neighborhood. The prevalence of cancer in the Black population had risen at nearly the same rate as the number of landfills and polluting industries that cropped up in poor Black neighborhoods across the country. Most of the people in the ER were Black. On protest nights like tonight the nurses said they usually were. To make matters worse, since The Taken violence against Black Americans had tripled nationwide. Those looking for an excuse had it and many others became understanding of their bigotry. Everyone else was held captive by the surrounding tide of hatred. Often its victims washed up at Grey Clinics. He had heard the horror stories from his classmates, but this was the first time Ezekiel had seen the carnage with his own eyes.

After weeks of reviewing medical charts Ezekiel knew that many North Birmingham residents were dying or would soon be dying of cancer. He also knew that the information Grey Corp gleaned from their genetic material would help prevent the same and other cancers in their richer neighbors and in other privileged people all over the country. Now, here the residents lay with dozens of others who had tried to fight on their behalf, battered and bleeding in the same clinic that profited from their misfortune. And Grey Corp had called Ezekiel and the other interns to come and take care of them while the doctors slept cozily in their beds.

Some of the patients wouldn't last the night. Ezekiel wondered bleakly how their neighborhood and others like it would survive in the shadow of so much industry and unrest. It seemed at times the new world was being built on top of them.

"Ezekiel!" Addie shouted from Room 2. He hurried inside where an elderly man lay curled up on the gurney. His arms flailed above him. Addie stood next to him with a hypodermic needle in one hand, trying to hold his wrist in the other.

"Mr. Martin. Please calm down, sir. This is just a sedative. It will help with the pain," Addie said.

Ezekiel approached the other side of the gurney and took hold of the man's arm as gently as he could. He slowly lowered it down to his side.

"Sir, we just want to help you," Addie said.

"Bullshit!" the man said. "I know what you people do."

"It's OK, sir," Ezekiel added.

Nurse Campbell appeared in the doorway.

"Mr. Martin, you forgot to sign your participation form." She walked over and stood next to Addie, tablet and e-pen in hand. Addie looked over at her, unable to hide her expression.

"Excuse me, Nurse, but we need to get him stabilized," Addie said.

Nurse Campbell smiled and pushed the tablet closer to Mr. Martin's face.

"We have to get a commitment from him before we can administer any care. Here you go Mr. Martin." She looked back at Addie with none of the warmth with which she'd favored Mr. Martin. "It's standard procedure, first sentence of your welcome packet."

Addie pursed her lips and looked over at Ezekiel. He met her gaze, trying to calm her without words. Slowly he released Mr. Martin's hand and took a step back. Addie lowered the needle and did the same.

"Why don't you two give us a moment?" Nurse Campbell said, smiling again. She pulled the stool up from the far wall and placed it next to the gurney. Taking a seat, she said "Now, now Mr. Martin this will all be over soon. Your–"

Addie stepped out the door first. Ezekiel closed it in disgust.

"I'm taking a break," Addie said and turned to the back exit. Before she made it there, a shriek of pain caught her attention and she hurried into Room 5.

For a brief moment Ezekiel missed school: the ease of their theories, the comfort of case studies and numbers, the relief of phylogenetics' distant perspective. Seeing people die out in front of your eyes held no such fascination, and he had no doubt he was watching the slow steady death knell of those who would not survive the new world. He felt he was standing at the breach, but briefly. Come morning he would return safely to the other side, out of this gap and moving on with the others.

Another wave of gurneys crashed through the entrance stunting the thought, but as Ezekiel tended to the people of Northern Birmingham he couldn't shake the feeling. By morning he could think of little else.

"What brings you to the middle of nowhere?"

Ezekiel looked over from the charts he was reviewing to Najit, one of the older interns who stood a few feet away, ignoring the reports on the tablet in front of him. After a short nap in Room 5, the supervising physician had handed them the results from the genetic samples they'd run the day before. Now they sat in a quiet corner of the clinic off-limits to participants and visitors, reviewing the aggregated data. With a touch of the pad, Ezekiel sent another analysis to a senior researcher in the lab.

"The same thing that brings you," Ezekiel answered. "The experience, learning."

"Hm," Najit said, continuing to stare at him. "I know who you are, you know," Najit said.

"Yes, we were introduced when I arrived. We haven't had any shifts together, but surely you haven't forgotten," Ezekiel said smiling tiredly.

"I mean I heard what you did," Najit said.

Ezekiel went back to reviewing the data in front of him.

"Hm," Najit repeated. Ezekiel ran his gaze over the chart. Too much red. Red represented an increase in the projected mortality rate of the North Birmingham population based on current disorder statistics.

"It's impressive, having come up with a new gene therapy technique at your age. What are you, sixteen? If I'd done it I'd never shut up about it. Trust me."

"I'm eighteen and I didn't come up with a new therapy, just suggested an updated technique for the existing one. You know that," he said, turning to Najit.

Najit smiled. "I do. Honest too. You could make a fortune with your insights if you were to go independent, you know. We're going to be best friends, I think Ezekiel."

Ezekiel shook his head and chuckled. Of course, he knew for-profit research could be quite lucrative. Ezekiel hadn't yet begun to fulfill his potential but sometimes he wondered what good it would do, giving the privileged even more privileges. Still, advanced genetics held very few other options; it was a consumer-based field. He exhaled and stretched his neck. Ezekiel was too tired for these Big Questions, as Addie called them. And where was she to save him from this conversation? That was a task partner: she worked and made the day fly by without resorting to odd passive-aggressive flattery.

"How about we just take it slow and see where it goes, Naj?" Ezekiel replied.

Najit smiled, revealing a single dimple. "Agreed."

The doorknob turned and Dr. Torson stepped in.

"Ezekiel, Najit, You can finish that later. You're needed up front." He strode back through the door into the main hallway. Ezekiel caught the door and held it for Najit.

"Now, to refresh, we accept calls for registered subjects only." He looked at Ezekiel meaningfully. "If they've contributed to the genetic registry here we can assist them medically for all injuries and conditions in Sections One and Two here," he said, handing them tablets. "Anything beyond this just tap this key here," he said as he finger hovered over a 'Reject/Eval' button on the tablet. "Any questions, direct them to Nurse Campbell or myself."

"Sorry, Dr. Torson, but life-threatening injuries as well, right?" Ezekiel asked.

"As of 6 am this morning we've reached out quota LTIs as well. Congratulations."

Ezekiel stared at Dr. Torson.

Ezekiel knew that the last public hospital in White County had closed six years earlier, and thus the agreement with Grey Corp – the only reason he'd chosen this particular clinic, far from the glamour and cachet of the top locations.

It took a moment to digest the information.

"Chin up, Carter. There are still people to be helped here," Dr. Torson said.

Those whose DNA Grey Corp had helped themselves to Ezekiel thought.

A phone rang at the dispatch desk. A few seconds later the call rang through to their tablets: a rural address at the edge of the county. The patient, thankfully, was an approved-care recipient, but instead of assigning it to him or Najit, Dr. Torson hit the Reject/Eval button.

"No need to waste any time on this one. A repeat offender," Dr. Torson said obliquely.

Just as he did, a disheveled Black man wearing a motorcycle helmet, torn jeans and a Green Bay Packers t-shirt burst through the front door.

"We need somebody. Don't ignore it," the biker said.

"Mr. Morton, as I have explained to you on more than one occasion– " Dr. Torson began.

"I'll take it," Ezekiel said.

Dr. Torson looked at him sharply. "Your time is not yours to waste."

"Could I take my break now then?" Ezekiel asked.

"You know what? Fine, Carter," he said glowering at him. "*I* will allow that. It's slow and this is a lesson you need to learn." He looked over at Najit and shook his head disapprovingly. Najit returned the expression. "Don't be late coming back. And you'll not take any clinic vehicles."

The biker nodded at Ezekiel. "You can ride with me."

Najit handed him a medical bag and Ezekiel followed the biker out into the sunny midday. The bike was parked on the curb just outside the door. The motorcycle wasn't what he expected – no retro chrome or cruiser replicas. It was a hunky dirt bike if anything. As Ezekiel climbed onto back of the ramshackle contraption - the damn thing ran on gas! - he began to understand, if not condone, his boss's decision. Before he could give it another thought, the biker tossed him a helmet and kicked the thing into life. Ezekiel steadied himself behind him and they sped out of the parking lot. Within minutes they hit a rough dirt road.

Dust flew up and stung Ezekiel's face. If he wasn't holding onto the back of the motorcycle seat for dear life as they zoomed over the pocked earth, he would have made some attempt at shielding his face, but as it was he just looked around the driver's head and squinted at the tall evergreens and battered houses they sped past. He should be in an air-conditioned lab breezing through the afternoon, but instead he found himself hurtling through a humid Alabama afternoon as recklessly as a fly drawn to shit.

They passed a barn nearly petrified with age and made a sharp left turn around it. Ezekiel strained every muscle in his body to stay on the bike and swore into the biker's ear. The biker yelled something back at Ezekiel, 'sorry' or 'so what', he couldn't be sure. The road smoothed out as they approached a residential property. The grass had been neatly trimmed on either side of the lane and ahead he could see the side of a bright blue farmhouse. The words 'Bird's Nest' were painted in wide, white, cursive letters between the first and second stories. Beyond the house, two large ramps were set up in a field next to a blue barn. Dozens of people milled around the area. As they rode closer, Ezekiel could see a set of silver bleachers at the edge of the field.

Ezekiel leaned in close to the biker's ear.

"Where's the patient?" he yelled.

"No patient yet."

"What?"

The biker sped toward the barn and stopped the bike short, throwing Ezekiel into him, and cut the engine. Ezekiel's ears rang in the sudden silence.

"You're on standby, Doc. She always hurts herself, so for once we wanted to be prepared. She's no spring chicken anymore."

Ezekiel looked at him incredulously.

"It's my mom, man," the biker said, throwing the kickstand down with his heel.

Ezekiel put his right leg down to steady his weight and got off the bike.

"Jump's in ten minutes," the biker said, "I'll have you back in 20. I promise." He looked at Ezekiel long enough to wait for some sort of confirmation. For the moment, the best Ezekiel could do was not to curse or refuse outright. Grudgingly Ezekiel nodded and headed toward the crowd.

"Thanks, man. We really appreciate it," the biker yelled at his back.

At least these people had some respect for him, Ezekiel thought as he neared the edge of the crowd. Old-school galvanized steel bleachers had been set up on the dusty patch of earth next to the blue barn. 'Lady Jay' had been painted on this building in the same extravagant letters, but here flecks of glitter lined the outside edge of the lettering, casting a bright rash of light over the dirt and across people's faces as they milled about, talking and sipping red, frosty beverages. Ezekiel coughed and looked around for their source. At the mouth of the barn he spied a long, narrow table; its wood had been burnished so that it nearly gleamed a rich red oak. There a man and woman poured the frothy concoction from two metal machines on the table. Ezekiel felt for his credit stick in his pocket and walked toward the table.

"On the house," the woman sang out before he reached them.

"I appreciate it, but–"

"Then just appreciate it," she replied.

Ezekiel nodded and took the drink from her hand. The chilled plastic felt pristinely cold and he took an eager sip – strawberries, nectarine, kiwi maybe, all of it refreshing and delicious.

"Thank you," he said. Inside the barn he could see framed photos nailed up to one side and a collection of dirt bikes that lined the walls. They sat in circles of overhead light. At the top of the wall of photos, black Western style letters, reading 'Lady Jay', were scorched into the wood. He couldn't quite make out the photographs and stepped closer to get a better look.

"You think that's old. Take a look at this."

Ezekiel turned to find a woman standing behind him. From her attire he could only assume she was Lady Jay. She wore the same white unitard and the flowing, bright blue cape in the photos. Smoky eye makeup and a shock of black in her otherwise short white afro proved it must be the same woman. He could see why she'd injured herself. Lady Jay looked much older than Ezekiel had imagined she would be. She was well-toned, with a line of sleek muscle visible in her arms and neck, but all that muscle was connected to bones that must be growing brittle with age.

"I'm sixty-eight," she said to the unspoken question.

Though his lips remained closed, Ezekiel's jaw actually dropped. He'd been thinking fifty-five. His face suddenly felt an inch longer, with the stretch from his bottom jaw to his arched eyebrows. Lady Jay broke up laughing.

"Oh child. Don't worry. I've been doing this near fifty years. I'll make it through the day."

"Ma'am, I have to advise against this," Ezekiel began. "A broken hip and the complications it causes can greatly reduce life expectancy."

She laughed in his face. "Is that how you talk to people, boy? I'll be fine and it's gotta be done."

"Why is that?"

"Why anything?" She looked at him more closely. "You are an earnest thing, ain't ya? Well, they see me jump this and then they wonder what they can do. Not all of them and not all the time but enough. The reason may change, but the effect is the same. It used to be cause I was Black or a woman or a mother. Now I'm all that plus I'm old." She paused. "Plus I think I'd just die of boredom otherwise." She laughed. "You might want to take a seat. The show's about to start."

Lady Jay turned and stepped away from him, further into the shadows of the barn.

Ezekiel walked out to the bleachers and sat down near the edge of the bottom row. It was the only seat left. He couldn't remember the last time he'd felt so nervous. His stomach started to hurt, and already he was practicing what he would say to Grey Corp when he had to call an ambulance in. His thoughts so consumed him that the sound of Lady Jay's engine kicking into gear made him jump. The throttle was high. He could feel the whining of it in his chest as well as in his ears. People around him hooted and clapped. As she emerged from the barn riding high atop her bike she was both an odd and spectacular sight. Under the helmet, the faceplate was large and crystal-clear, Lady Jay's wide smile visible through the plexi. She raised one arm and waved as she pulled out of the shadows and into the bright sun.

Ezekiel looked over at the ramps. They seemed to have doubled in size in the last few minutes and now looked impossibly tall, the distance between them far too great. He peered more closely at the ramps, studying the angle of incline, trying to imagine how this woman would make the jump.

Lady Jay waved once more at the crowd and gunned her engine, barreling toward the other side of the property. As she shrank into a distant figure and then a dark dot, whispered excitement rose up from the folks on the bleachers. Ezekiel strained to see Lady Jay clearly. He squinted and looked forward. Finally she turned and stopped near the turnoff from the road. As she stopped, she put one booted foot down on the ground, and sat. The sound of the engine was distant and low. The people around him quieted, all heads turned to the extreme left as they waited.

The throttle shot up. The engine of Lady Jay's motorcycle caught on the wind and the sound roared toward them. Here she came. First a dot and then more, the engine whining as she advanced. She sped closer and became a person again. Ezekiel could clearly see the writing on her jumpsuit, the bright blue and white on her bike. As she neared the ramp, Lady Jay stood up on the on the pegs, like an equestrian leading her steed to the steeple. She hit the ramp straight on. Ezekiel's chest tightened, watching her cross in front of him.

When Lady Bird's back tire left the first ramp, time slowed to match her transformation.

It shouldn't have worked. Ezekiel knew how to perform complex gene therapies while his peers were casting their first votes; he had lost his parents and his Grandma Maddie, leaving him to walk alone and find his way through the world; the country teetered at the edge of a race war and a class war; every day saw religious skirmishes, food insecurity and a general distrust of one another. So it shouldn't have been possible for Lady Bird to ensnare Ezekiel and the rest of the crowd in her magic. She shouldn't have been capable of inspiring wonder. Wonder itself was a naïve notion from a distant time and certainly shouldn't result from a gas-powered relic crossing from one wooden wedge to another, delaying gravity for a few scant seconds in between.

But it did.

Perhaps it was the improbability that catapulted it past entertainment and into something more.

Ezekiel sat on the aluminum bleachers, a smile plastered across his face as he watched her.

Lady Bird hung in the air – suspended . . . floating . . . flying. Her blue cape billowed out behind her; her hair encircled her like a crown. Her expression was triumphant, both peaceful and riveted, as if all of life coursed through her and it took this feat for others to see that.

She carried their wonder into the heavens and in the bright sunshine it shone.

And she was right. Watching her, Ezekiel realized what more he could do. With his genetic genius, he could lift those left behind and propel them over the breach. But for the moment he simply sat in awe.

First Born

If Ezekiel couldn't turn her, the baby would die. He stood at the foot of the gurney, wrist deep in another human being, wishing for a moment like he hadn't since he was a boy. He took a deep breath and wished for a steady hand to do what the obstetrician had failed to. And that he himself had studied deliveries as intensely as genetics.

If the baby died, no one would ever get reparations.

Then the breath was over and he had to find a way.

Dr. Ezekiel Carter adjusted his hands, prayed under his breath and turned the child with a strength for which he would later apologize. The baby girl shifted and slowly revolved.

She was born forty minutes later.

Her mother named her Opal Zekia – Opal after an aunt who had died in the Rep War, and Zekia in honor of Dr. Carter. Opal, the first baby to receive genetic reparations, weighed six pounds and four ounces. She was no bigger or smaller than the other babies in the nursery.

Ezekiel stood just inside the doorway, watching her. To look at her, one couldn't have picked her out of the crowd. He couldn't see the difference between Opal and the other children sleeping and stirring in their incubators, but she was different. The other newborns might have had gene work done – it had become common enough – but he knew it was nothing like Opal's.

Ezekiel had designed the Center and its program to not only provide prenatal genetic adaptations for those who couldn't afford it, but to provide adaptations designed by one of the most talented geneticists on the planet. His adaptations were empirically superior. Opal would have health beyond what was available on the open market; she would be exceptional.

Though genetic adaptations were a matter of probability and possibility, Ezekiel felt an utter certainty about, if not who, how this child would be: Her body would react to the environment and regulate its own existence with an unparalleled efficiency and rigor. He had seen to it – for 18 hours of every day for the last 10 months and all the years of research and preparation, he had used his genius, done the work and now he had made something right. The factories producing toxins more quickly than their wares and the country's history of inequality and upheaval would never be. But now it need not be; Ezekiel had put the power back in the present and back in people's hands.

A few feet away from where he stood, three new fathers beamed with pride as they looked through the plexiglass. Ezekiel doubted very much that they felt the way he did in that moment – wondered even if he would have felt such a swell in his chest at his own child's birth. He wouldn't ever know that feeling – science did have its limitations – but he doubted it could feel any better than this.

He should get home; he'd almost forgotten about the day's earlier excitement, but now it was time to check on Dear Heart and Quincy. After a few more minutes watching Opal and going over the details of her transfer back to the Center at the end of her observation period, he left the hospital and drove the short ride back to the Center for a final check-in with Addie. As he entered the building, Ezekiel walked past the rooms of the other third-trimester mothers. He took the time to look in on them and flash a friendly face so that they would know everything had gone well.

Addie met him halfway to her office with a warm smile. She still wore her lab whites. The sleeves were rolled up to her elbows, a bright red pen stuck out of the dark bun of her hair. He shook his head; he couldn't believe she still carried a pen. 'It's only obsolete until the electricity goes out' she'd told him once.

"I've got this shift, Ezekiel," she said, squeezing his shoulder. He pulled her in for a brief hug. It was only the third time they'd hugged, the others being at his Grandma Maddie's funeral and Addie's commitment ceremony, but this day was just as momentous.

"We did it, Addie," he said, pulling back.

"You did it – well actually she did it." She chuckled.

"That OB–" he started.

"Already taken care of. He's on his way to back to Chicago as we speak."

"You were right. He was the wrong choice," Ezekiel said.

Addie's smiled widened. "You do like to see the best in people, Ezekiel. Dr. Gerald is still available," she said.

"Lucky for us. Would you give him the call?"

"Of course. Now, go get some rest and let Dear Heart know how everything went. I know she wanted–" Addie stopped herself and looked up at Ezekiel apologetically. "Sorry."

"No, you're right. I'm sure it's killing her that she couldn't be here. I messaged her just after the delivery, but it's time to give her a full rundown."

"Is everything OK now? Is Quincy OK?" she asked.

Ezekiel thought for a second of sharing his honest answer, reconsidered.

"She said he's fine. I'm sure he was as soon as she got there." Ezekiel scratched the space just above his right ear. "Quincy only listens to her lately so really it's best she handled it. Still, it would have meant a lot. After all she recruited Ms. Baker."

Addie nodded in agreement. "All of our candidates."

"We should both be able to make it in tomorrow though," he said.

"It's been a long day. Are you OK to drive? Maybe a service would be better?" she asked.

"I'll be fine. The drive will do me good." He paused, looking at his friend.

"Thank you, Addie. For everything." He grinned and turned toward the exit. "I'll see you in the morning."

"Try the afternoon."

"Now who's working too much?" Ezekiel said.

They chuckled, each heading a separate way.

"In the morning," he called over his shoulder as he reached the exit. He entered his code into the lock pad. The door hissed open.

The night air cooled him as he stepped out into the parking lot. He turned his face toward the waning moon, and inhaled. The distant fragrance of magnolia soothed him.

"Blasphemer!"

The woman popped out of a car in the back row, just to the left of Ezekiel's sterling luxury sedan. An older woman in her late 60s or 70s, she wore a bright white choir robe that contrasted with her dark skin, but matched the hair pulled back in an unruly puff.

A robe, really? Ezekiel thought tiredly.

"Heathen!" she yelled at him as she unsteadily advanced.

Ezekiel clenched his jaw and started toward his car.

"Heathen! You can't run from God!" the woman screamed at his back.

"You ma'am, are not God," Ezekiel replied without turning.

"Neither are you! Messing with those most sacred! Trying to do God's work!"

Ezekiel reached the car, unlocked it, and closed the door behind him quickly. As he pulled out of the lot and onto the main road, he watched the white robe recede into the darkness. The sound of her yelling faded into the distance.

The trip home on the interstate was a long bright ride. Though just a few light posts lined the roadway with their dim orange glow, electronic billboards the size of houses hovered in the black, hawking everything from attorneys to secure housing complexes nestled behind guard towers and taser fences. Many of the billboards were for bio adaptations – genetic prenatal as well as the popular body modifications that had replaced plastic surgery in the last decade. One billboard in particular always caught Ezekiel's eye.

'Your Dream Child Awaits', it said. Next to the slogan a huge embryo rendered in neon stood out on an otherwise black background. Above the billboard holograms of a perfect future radiated out from the space between the words and image: a beautiful home, a graduate's cap, and awards all etched in the night sky like glittering fireworks that never burned out. It made Ezekiel shake his head each evening as he passed it. 'Your dream child awaits', he thought derisively. If only it were so simple, like ordering a meal. If it were, he wouldn't want anything to do with crafting every nuance of individuality out of a person – as if upbringing, environment, and just the damn person were irrelevant.

Ezekiel turned off the main road, leaving the bright lights behind him. Holly hedges lined the long driveway, creating a tunnel that his car moved through. He always loved this last stretch of asphalt before he got home. Ezekiel opened the windows and the din of cicadas filled the cabin. Just visible through the trees he spied the light from the kitchen windows. Yawning, he turned into the driveway, watched the garage door sensor light up, and waited for the door to lift.

Inside the house, Ezekiel could hear the quiet tones of Dear Heart on the phone in the kitchen. The lights in the foyer and living room were out. He placed his bag next to the door and followed the light, the sound of his wife's voice. He could smell the remnants of dinner. As Ezekiel rounded the corner, Quincy almost ran straight into him. The boy stopped himself short just in time.

"Hey Q," Ezekiel said, reaching out to touch the top of the seven-year-old's head. Quincy dodged his hand and moved swiftly to the stairwell.

From where Dear Heart stood at the kitchen counter, she turned and covered the bottom of the receiver with her hand.

"Uh uh, Quincy. Come back here," she said, pointing at one of the kitchen chairs. "Sit down."

A half-finished plate of mashed potatoes, greens, and snapper waited on the table just in front of it. It was still going on then, Ezekiel thought to himself. No doubt, he'd need to talk to him about it, but first he had to get more details from Dear Heart. He looked over at the clock: 9:30 and she was still on the phone about it.

Quincy sat down in the chair Dear Heart had pointed out. He stared at the ground. Had he cheated? Ezekiel wondered, maybe a fight? Dear Heart had told him scant details on the phone – no doubt to keep him focused on the day's work, but she was pissed, still. Whatever Quincy had done it had to be worse than usual.

Their son had been to the best schools with the most awarded teachers but always found a way not to learn his lesson. When he paid attention he did well on tests, but that was only after the administration suggested moving him to a different program. On both of those occasions, Quincy had performed well. Ezekiel couldn't help but think of it that way: performing.

He sometimes wondered about Quincy's biological father. Was he a performer as well? Some sort of actor? When they met, Dear Heart would only say the man was a mistake from her past, and one that would stay in the past. Ultimately it didn't matter; Quincy was his son and Ezekiel's absence must be the cause, not what the other man had contributed. Ezekiel had vowed to be there for his child as his father had not been for him. He sighed, rubbing at a pang of guilt that seized the side of his torso. As he finished his dinner, Quincy still wouldn't look at him. His eyes had moved up to the tabletop but no further.

Dear Heart ended her conversation with a last apology and hung up. She kept her back to them as she reached out to the counter in front of her and leaned for a moment. A heavy sigh escaped her.

"Quincy, go upstairs," she said.

He did as he was told. As the boy passed Ezekiel, his gaze flickered up to him and Ezekiel held eye contact for a moment, not sure whether to give him a faint smile or something sterner. Still undecided, he watched his son climb the stairs.

Dear Heart turned and mustered a weary smile. Ezekiel crossed the small distance between them and held her in a loose embrace.

"Z," she began, "I want to hear all about your magnificent day. Every last second of it, but first I need to tell you what he did."

"What is it?" he asked.

"Today, he had a man arrested, a man who had done nothing."

"What?" The word came out sharp.

"A man who works at the corner store near the school. He caught Quincy stealing, so he called the cops and took Quincy in the back to wait for them."

"The cops?" Ezekiel said disbelievingly.

"Apparently this wasn't the first time he'd caught him stealing. He'd warned Quincy before. He had even tried to call his parents, but Quincy gave him a made-up number."

Where the hell had he been? Ezekiel wondered.

"When the cops got there," she continued, "Quincy told them that the man had touched him."

"What?!" Ezekiel took a half-step back. "He touched him?!"

"No. He didn't," she said quietly.

"What? How, how do you know that?"

"Quincy said the guy had done it while they were in the back. Apparently he was very convincing. The cops arrested the guy and they called us. By the time I got to the station and could see straight, the man was nearly crying, totally freaked out. After he got it together, he remembered that the store has surveillance for that room."

Ezekiel waited for the rest.

"They reviewed the footage, and showed it to me. Ezekiel, he didn't touch him. He put one hand on his shoulder to lead him into the room and never touched him again."

"But–" Ezekiel began.

"Quincy admitted it," she said. "Spat it out like it was somebody else's fault."

A crash erupted from upstairs. They turned and hurried toward the noise. Ezekiel beat Dear Heart up the stairwell and to Quincy's room. He flung the door open and there Quincy lay on the floor next to his computer, both hands clasped around his knee. A grimace of pain pinched his features into a tight ball.

"What happened? Are you okay?" Ezekiel asked. Keeping his gaze on Quincy, Ezekiel leaned away from the door frame and asked Dear Heart to grab his medical bag from the foyer.

As soon as Ezekiel moved, the expression on Quincy's face evaporated. The boy looked up past the shelf above his desk and at the ceiling, not just calm, but detached. Quincy must have thought Ezekiel couldn't see him, and in truth Ezekiel did not recognize the boy. The boy who used to lie on his chest and fall asleep, who had called him Daddy and never Ezekiel, who had held his hand when there was no street to cross, was not the person in front of him.

"Quincy?" Ezekiel said apprehensively.

This boy started. He turned and looked at Ezekiel with annoyance just visible in the tight downturned corners of his mouth. Ezekiel thought the boy's eyes might have looked softer, searching. But he couldn't be sure. Looking at his son, Ezekiel wondered for the first time, not who this child would be, but who he was.

A small, thin, white square fell from the shelf above Quincy's desk. As it flipped in its descent, Ezekiel noticed a photograph on it and could clearly read: Roswell Police Department.

Just then, Dear Heart walked up behind him and put the medical bag in his open hand. She scooted past him and into the room.

Opal

Opal's mother, Lill, bragged that weeds were jealous of how quickly her daughter grew. But they had never done it so beautifully. Opal's white teeth sparkled behind thick, pink gums. Her tan skin was so clear and smooth that she seemed to be lit from within. A crown of full black hair hovered around her face, radiating softly. When Opal and her mother waited in the food line at Piedmont Park, people who'd been standing under the Georgia sun for hours asked if they could hold her, so strong was their desire to touch her vitality.

Not everyone felt that way.

On one of their few visits, Opal's aunt and grandmother sat on the living room couch, watching her play with her older cousin, Monika, who had just turned two.

Monika was six months older, but the two girls were nearly the same size. Like their mothers, they sat next to each other, Monika dressed in a cranberry jumper and Opal in a green apple dress. They had the same full lips and pointed eyebrows, but Monika's perfect newness had begun to fade as she toddled into childhood; in Opal, it remained.

Dozens of bright plastic blocks covered the floor around the girls. They took turns building and destroying towers. Opal worked with an excited smile, pushing the blocks into place as Monika stood up to build higher.

Their grandmother pulled a cigarette out of the pocketbook at her feet, and looked away.

She sucked her teeth and frowned with one side of her mouth, bringing out a dimple that just now looked like a dent. Ratty hair extensions swung across the nape of her neck as she turned to Opal's mother and lit her cigarette.

"She's a little full of herself ain't she?" Opal's grandmother said.

Lill glanced over, the corners of her mouth turned down.

"Aren't they all at this age?" she answered.

"Monika ain't."

Lill looked at Monika. The girl had shoved half of her fist into her mouth. Her other hand picked up each block in Opal's tower and threw it towards the other side of the room. Opal watched her cousin, giggling.

"Already showing sins. You need to get that child in a church," Opal's grandmother said, exhaling a cloud of smoke. She pulled her jacket tighter around her and hummed her dissatisfaction.

Lill protested: "She's not even eighteen months yet. And Opal's *been* baptized."

"What you trying to say, Lill?" Opal's grandmother answered. "I know that. Besides, dipping her in water can't wash off the taint. It's *in* her," the old woman pursed her lips and shook her head. "You made sure of that."

Lill had wondered when her family would start. They didn't care that the biogenetic adaptations had improved Opal's health to levels far beyond the norm, didn't want her to have that fighting chance, couldn't appreciate this strength even in a time when the cases of dengue and yellow fever rose with the temperature. It didn't matter to them that Dr. Carter's reparations were the only ones anyone ever received.

"What? We ain't good enough for you?" Opal's grandmother said. "You got to change what we is. Learn how to be humble before God and life would have no pain."

While her grandmother spoke, Opal's aunt walked over to the girls and picked Monika up. She returned to the couch and held the girl in her lap, wiped away a trail of snot that had escaped from Monika's nose.

"It ain't natural what she is," her aunt added.

Oblivious to her words, Opal beamed at her, giggles bubbling up into laughter.

•

Before Opal, her mother hardly heard laughter. Everyone's life had gone grim in those decades – or, more specifically, everyone on the bottom. By the end of 2030, there was no middle class – only the bottom and a thin film of prosperous individuals on top. The effects of global warming, both financial and physical, had heated the classes up until they separated. Opal's mother called it the shit bucket economy. She often pictured it as she stood in the work lines on Peachtree, the food lines in Five Points. The lines had grown as she had grown, until the occasional trip as a child became the weekly ritual of adulthood.

Only prisons prospered – prisons and conglomerates. Black people filled the former, barely dotted the latter.

Moderates called it aftershocks from the failed battle for reparations. Militants claimed such conditions had caused the Rep War.

The old folks said it was like time had stopped and went backwards to match people's minds.

From where Lill stood it all seemed inevitable. Everything bad seemed inevitable – even her new pregnancy.

So when Dr. Carter's wife, Dear Heart, approached her while she waited, full-bellied and hungry in the food line, and asked if she wanted to give her child a better chance, Lill agreed to be the first.

•

Opal started kindergarten without having had a single cold. Lill, proud and pleased, explained that she stayed healthy because of the gift Dr. Carter had given her.

•

Just after Opal turned ten, the epiflu hit the East Coast. She saw the first report on the tram ride home from school. By the time she'd curled up on the couch for a snack, New York had 1,000 new cases. Though far from fatal, it looked to Opal that the sick people on the screen with their bloodshot eyes and distended purple lips would just as soon be dead.

The flu swept into Atlanta the second week of November. From the first day, students in her class shot germs at each other in coughs and sneezes. By the time school officials called for an early holiday vacation, Opal had the substitute teachers nearly all to herself.

•

Opal couldn't see the golden sheen that surrounded her desk, but the other kids sure as hell did. They scrutinized every inch of it as Mrs. Harris, the history teacher, prattled on about the beginnings of the Rep War. She spoke in the haughty tones of one who had lived through a time and now had the distinct pleasure of becoming a primary resource. Every once in a while she closed her teacher's edition, as she did now, and lectured, the annals of her memory coughing up details that the textbook had left out.

"After The Taken, it became a shooting war. But, really, what could anyone expect after *that*?"

The children weren't listening. Behind their pox scars and still swollen lips they watched Opal sit pristine before them, her breath even and steady as they rattled the last of epiflu out of their chests.

Opal had sent out 'get well' cards and welcomed each of her classmates back as they returned. When she found out that Tasha Scott's family had lost both grandfather and baby cousin to the pandemic, her mother sent flowers with their condolences. Now Tasha hunkered over her desk in the back of the room, gaze fixed on Opal's back. Opal couldn't differentiate Tasha's cold stare from anyone else's. She felt them all heating her from behind. But Opal kept her head up, smiled when someone met her gaze.

Still, her health offended them: her eternal health, like an ache in their chests.

•

Soon after, Opal stopped growing. That night her mother stood next to the front door, slowly unwinding a scarf from her neck while Opal started dinner in the kitchen. Lill stared at the air in front of her, hands trembling from more than cold.

As Opal dug for mushrooms in the moist soil of the bottom bin, a subtle sound distracted her. She stopped digging and heard:

"Opal, come sit," softly.

She preferred to keep digging until the bad news that had quieted her mother passed. Still, she came into the living room and settled into the warm spot she'd earlier made on the careworn couch. Her mother sat next to her.

A cone of yellow light from the overhead lamp shone straight down into her mother's hair. It picked the gray strands out from the rest and tried to hypnotize Opal with them while her mother sidled up to what she intended to say.

"Did you watch the net today?" her mother asked.

"Some," Opal answered.

"A boy was attacked in Doraville."

"Yeah, I saw that." Opal looked up at her mother. For a brown-skinned woman she was ashen.

"Well, they did an update while I was riding home."

The corners of her mother's mouth turned down, pushing the skin into sharp creases. Only one thing brought on that expression. Opal waited for her to say it.

"He was like you, the boy." Her mother paused and met her gaze. "His friends did that to him," she said.

Opal held her breath in the space between her mouth and nose, temporarily forgetting how to breathe for a moment.

"Not his friends, I guess, but some of the other students."

•

Opal sat in widower's row, the back pew, far away from the other children. She shared the bench with a few old men, gray and curled as ashes. Though the sun beaming through the window beat down the neck of her gray dress, she sat still and listened to the pastor try to raise the spirit by way of raising interest in raising funds for their sister church in Savannah. Somebody had bombed it the week before. Everyone knew why, but no one would say it.

They held their tongues and nodded at the preacher's word, but an unmistakable discomfort filled the church that morning. Opal tried to pass it off as heat and closeness.

For once, she had been looking forward to church. At her grandmother's insistence, Sunday morning always found Opal in a pew. Most days, like today, her mother had to work, but that didn't release her from the promise. But after spending the whole week alone in the apartment, Opal appreciated the chance to be with other people.

So she sat in the back of the church in a drab dress that had the impossible effect of making her just as, if not more, radiant.

Every once in a while a boy from her school twisted around in his seat and glowered at her. Then Tasha Scott would turn and regard her coolly. To Opal, it seemed nearly choreographed so that three minutes couldn't pass without someone turning and looking at her.

They would have looked anyway, but today they had a special reason. Opal knew as well as they did: the Savannah church had been attacked because of the two Carter Kids in its congregation.

Opal stared straight ahead. She tried to collapse her vision into a tunnel so that everything around the pastor's face blurred into an unrecognizable collection of colorful blots.

The pastor hung his head low, one fist resting against the podium.

"Brothers and sisters, as we reach into our hearts for charity we must remember that a new threat is in our midst."

Heads nodded. An electric current began to build up from the corners of the room. Women in the middle said "Amen," requested that the pastor "speak on it!"

"Gone are the days when a person simply was what he was. Today, people are changing their *children*!"

"Have mercy," from the signifiers in the front row.

The man next to Opal shifted in his seat, opening a space between his hip and hers.

"Today! Men seek to be God!"

"Amen! Jesus!" from a woman in a peach dress just a few pews in front of Opal.

Waves of nausea moved across Opal's abdomen. The heat on her neck opened up to a full-on blaze. Her feet slid across sweat trapped in her scuffed suede slippers. She looked up. The pastor's eyes bore into her. His mouth made an obscene 'O' as the sermon swelled over his paunch and washed over the congregation.

"These things cannot be abided!"

The kids in front were looking back in bunches now. She felt them, ready to hurry to the church doors so they could throw mean words at her back.

Maybe they would only throw words.

The thought hushed her, for two heartbeats.

Opal sprang out of her seat and ran through the thick wooden doors, down the street. She made it to the tram just before the doors closed. Heading for an empty seat across the aisle, Opal didn't look up until the tram chugged forward.

A group of kids dominated the middle of the car, talking and laughing. In their long black jackets and custom cuts, they looked a lot like the kids at Opal's school, probably the kids at any school.

Peering closer, she saw how faded they looked. Saw the shadows of circles already under their eyes. How their skin exploded into welts and pimples. The raised scar on a collarbone, above an eyebrow.

But she looked too long. They began to turn in her direction.

Opal hunched down in her seat, stared at the floor, shrinking by her own will.

The Ghost of Kristen Burke

Kristen only wanted to see her sister. Sarcoma was taking Marilu away, so Kristen had crossed 9,000 miles to hold her hand, look in her younger sister's face and say goodbye. If her fellow passengers had recognized her, they would think that Kristen Burke, indelible symbol of the Rep War, had come back from the dead. The well-dressed men and women sharing business class didn't seem to be aware of her resurrection. Most dozed in their high-backed seats, perhaps dreaming of the ground now only forty-five minutes away.

Kristen was the only one of The Taken who had actually made it to Africa. The other children of senators abducted by the radical group New Dawn had safely returned to American soil. No one in the U.S. outside her family and a tight group of security insiders knew what became of Kristen. Eventually the media seemed to forget about her, if not her image. They had that – the visage of her terrorized and broken, broadcast by New Dawn – and their rage.

She didn't look much like the newspaper photos anymore. Two decades as a dead legend had left dark crescent moons under her eyes. The sun had lightened her hair to a shade of red that the nineteen-year-old Kristen would have hated. Already, age spots colored her skin, telling of the hours spent in the bright Seychellen sun outside her home, gathering rocks to pretty the small garden she kept just outside her front door. She often used the garden as a backdrop for her self-portraits. Kristen loved the house and her privacy as she did few other things, having reserved most of her affection for the people and places she captured in her photos. They became the home she had left behind.

That was the deal she was given fifteen years before: she could stay away and her family would support her as long as no one knew her fate. Kristen hadn't known why and she hadn't cared. She only knew what had happened to her and that the whole world had seen. Her family's love could not change that or mend the wounds that New Dawn had inflicted. She didn't want to trouble her family with her madness, a madness she was sure would pass, but only in isolation.

So she retreated to a place without mirrors or reminders of a life that was now lost to her. But she had also resolved to come back knowing who this new woman was, and how she could live in her infamy.

Kristen still didn't know, but Marilu's illness wouldn't wait, hence she hurtled 600 miles per hour back to the land of her birth.

On the ground, Kristen felt like she'd landed in the future. The Seychelles dabbled in technology: handhelds were ubiquitous enough, but beyond that it prided itself on its low-tech island lifestyle and Seychellois would have to go to one of the tourist hotels to find the level of gadgetry she saw here. She'd been reacquainted with holo advertisements as they stalked her during the Johannesburg layover, but this onslaught of bright lights and bevy of conglom-sponsored virtual reality lounges was another world indeed. Cautiously, she moved through the crowds in the airport. So many people. Praslin wouldn't have half this many people on the island during high tourist season. A small girl ambled by, barely visible in the rush of bodies. Kristen looked around for the child's parents and spotted a man who watched the girl as he casually talking on his handheld a dozen yards away. Kristen shook her head and kept moving. When she reached the baggage claim it was chaotic and close. With some effort, she waited for her two blue suitcases to emerge from the recesses of the airport. Excusing herself she grabbed them quickly and walked outside where she saw a dark sedan idling on the curb. Near it, a middle-aged man, an agent she guessed by his ramrod posture, held a sign with the name "Bubba" on it. She smiled at Marilu's sense of humor and approached him. As she did, another man emerged from the car.

Agents' dress code must have changed in the intervening years or perhaps it was an attempt at casual dress. These agents wore khaki-colored pants and light sweaters. They had the same telltale bulges just under their arms – just like the impersonator who had plucked her off the street near campus all those years ago. As one of the men approached, the day felt hotter, the air prickly. Kristen looked up at him, and her vision blurred at the edges. Her breath quickened and caught. She stared at a small silver pin, a monogram, on his lapel. She focused on that tiny shining 'KBS', willing herself to stay in the present, pushing back the phantom smell of sweat, the ringing in her ears.

"Ma'am," he said, "It's a honor to meet you. We've come to escort you."

Kristen nodded her head grimly and made herself walk to the sedan. Though her shoulders trembled slightly, her eyes were steady as the sea after a storm.

As they rode, Kristen kept testing the door locks in the car. The open window blew frigid air straight into her face, long hair churning across her vision. She grazed the top of the window frame with her left hand. Her right kept returning to the lock to click it open, shut, open, shut while they drove through the dawn streets.

When they arrived at Marilu's grand Tudor estate thirty minutes later and slid through the front gate, Kristen clicked the lock open one more time. She didn't wait for the driver to open her door as they came to a stop. She got out and kept a wide space between them as she moved toward the trunk. She smiled faintly at him before taking her bags from his outstretched hands.

"Thank you, but this will do. You can go," she said. Kristen watched until the sedan ambled around the circular drive and disappeared down the street. When she could no longer see the car, she walked past the manicured tulips to the massive front door and rang the bell. An old fashioned chime rang out. Birds twittered above her as she waited for someone to answer.

Marilu's husband, David, opened the door. A few inches shorter than Kristen, he appeared the consummate casual aristocrat. He wore a light beige sweater, linen slacks, and thick cotton socks. A full head of curly brown hair completed the look.

"Kristen," he said stretching out his hand. "It's wonderful to finally meet you in person." He grinned.

She took his hand and returned the smile. Marilu had chosen wisely. His grip was gentle, but strong, his gaze clear and friendly. Kristen pulled him in for a brief hug.

"Thank you for taking care of my baby sister," she replied. "May I see her?"

"Of course." He took her bags and closed the heavy door behind her. "She's been waiting for you. Our room is back here now." He swept his arm toward a long hallway behind the large oak staircase just beyond the foyer and its soaring ceiling. Kristen's footsteps rang out on the marble floors.

She stepped through the open bedroom door. Inside, Marilu was lovely and cracked and dying. Kristen could see that as soon as she entered the room. The quilt that covered Marilu lay flat where her lower left leg had been and Kristen put her hand on the emptiness as she leaned down to kiss her. She placed her cheek against Marilu's, feeling the dryness, but also the warmth of her skin.

"Ox," she said, whispering Marilu's childhood name.

"Bub," her sister replied.

Kristen could not move away. She shifted her weight, and instead of sitting on the chair next to the bed, she brought her legs up and nestled around Marilu, hugging her sister. They cried quietly together.

In a few moments, Kristen felt Marilu's breathing ease, and realized she was asleep. She joined her sister in slumber and sometime later woke to a light scratching across her forehead. Upon opening her eyes, she found Marilu watching her through a watery, peaceful gaze. Marilu moved a lock of hair off of her forehead.

"You look so different," Marilu said.

"I am different."

"Not where it counts, never there." Her gaze drifted to the window. "Hey Bub, take a trip with me?" Marilu asked.

"Anywhere."

•

Reclining in a set of adirondack chairs far into the gardens behind the house, Kristen, Marilu and David enjoyed the cool breeze blowing through the trees as they finished their picnic. The sun was gentle, all light and just enough heat to warm the fertile scene that surrounded them.

"Lovely," Marilu said. "I haven't been back here in ages."

"She wouldn't come for me, Kristen," David said playfully.

Marilu reached over and took his hand.

"I thought those KBS idiots were still hounding the grounds," Marilu said.

"KBS? What's that? What does it stand for?" Kristen asked.

Marilu and David exchanged a look.

"It stands for the Kristen Burke Society," Marilu answered.

The color drained out of Kristen's face.

"And what the hell is that?" she asked.

"You didn't hear of it at all?" David asked. He looked at her, caught her expression. "Sorry, this is going to come as a shock." He paused. "But it's a lynch mob, effectively. A well-funded, nearly sanctioned lynch mob. They started showing up in the news with demonstrations and recruiting drives when I was still doing my post-doc. Members of Congress joined. They've been linked to suspicious murders, racketeering, alliances with supremacist groups, everything. And the sons of bitches have even lurked around here."

Kristen could hear what he was saying, but there was a delay, a second of incomprehension before each new fact registered.

"It started just after, Kristen," Marilu added. "Daddy would never admit it, but I think he had something to do with it. He was so enraged, you can't imagine it. But it got away from him. Of course it did. You can't control mad dogs."

"Tell me everything," Kristen said.

David picked up his handheld and spoke near the corner of it.

"Kristen Burke Society," he said and handed it to her.

A sea of type stood out on the screen and Kristen began to read. With each new act of violence she read, waves of emotion crashed over her wall of hard-fought peace.

She felt comfort wash away and in its place came something empty and small. She knew this feeling. She knew it better than trust or comfort or relief. She knew it better than the name they'd used to justify the unjustifiable, to smother justice in her private pain.

Kristen stayed up that night and acquainted herself with the full measure of the Kristen Burke Society.

By 3 am, she couldn't read anymore. She sat and stared into space, considering. She had not passed the oppressive legislation of KBS senators or looked the other way when Klan Riders terrorized towns in the Delta. She hadn't spouted rhetoric laced with violent racism or intimidated people into giving up their right to be different and still free. She had done nothing.

She had done nothing.

•

Kristen took her morning coffee with Marilu, and when her little sister dozed off to sleep, she asked David for a phone and took a long walk out in the gardens.

She made two demands for her interview. It had to be live and as soon as possible. Forty-eight hours later she sat in a Victorian chair in front of a fake fireplace with cameras trained on her, beaming out her visage to homes across the country.

"Kristen Burke," the host said in hushed tones. "Welcome back."

"Thank you," Kristen replied.

"Tell us, Kristen. Where have you been?" the host asked dramatically. Her brows were knitted together, head cocked to one side, looking for the moment like an inquisitive cat.

"Oh, I'm sorry," Kristen said. "I won't be answering any questions. I just wanted to tell you all something." She looked intently at the host and leaned in a bit. "You're the ones who've been kidnapped. Your future's stolen. Phillip Tailor, that awful Burke society, and your own fear some of you and your own hate some others," she looked directly into the camera, "they've mastered you."

"Kristen—," the host tried to butt in. Kristen continued.

"I'm free now and you're in a cage." She started to stand and abruptly sat back down, turning back to the camera. "And Kristen Burke . . . that's *my* name. It's *mine*. *They* didn't even try to take my name so you did them one better. But you can't have it. You hear me? You can't have it and you can't hide behind it. Or me."

Kristen stared through the lens for a second more and then slowly stood. On her second step, she stumbled but quickly regained her grace. She felt the camera following her as she opened the door and left the room.

Behind her, the host began to speak hurriedly. The woman could say whatever gibberish she wanted; Kristen had said her piece.

Out on the street, she made a mental note to ask David how to take a screen shot of the interview. She would add it to her self-portrait collection, but first she wanted to see for herself how she looked at her homecoming.

Once Removed

Dear Heart lay awake with her eyes closed, exhausted from her sleepless night and the thoughts that would not leave her be. She felt the dampness of a stubborn tear touching the inside of her ear. It would not dry, had not had time to, but the soft morning sun glowing beyond the bedroom shades said that it must, that her feelings had to retreat. No one must know. Or perhaps they should, she wavered again. Regardless, she thought, now was not the time if there were to be such a time.

She felt Ezekiel stir at her back. Turning her head, she rolled into her pillow and hid her expression while he moved gently off the mattress and onto the floor. She could hear him as he padded to the bathroom and softly closed the door behind him. Dear Heart stayed in bed long after he'd peed his long fretful morning pee and dressed – so long that he now stood in the bathroom doorway looking down at her. She knew this though she hadn't opened her eyes. The sound of his movements had slowed and stopped in front of her. Now, the flesh on the side of her face prickled with the weight of his gaze. This feeling, of being watched by a man, wasn't new to her though it was one of the few times Ezekiel had done it.

"Are you OK?" he asked, his voice low. Dear Heart opened her eyes and looked up at him. Ezekiel walked to the edge of the bed and sat down next to her, laid one hand on her arm.

"You looked stressed," he said.

It took three deep breaths before she could respond in anything like a normal tone of voice. Then she lied to him for the first time in nine years.

"I'm fine," she said. Ezekiel continued to look at her with concern. He caressed the skin on her upper arm with his thumb, waiting. Dear Heart sat up and hugged him tightly, saying with her embrace what she couldn't otherwise.

He squinted, looking at her more closely. He looked down to her chin and back up. Dear Heart took a breath.

"Why don't you and Quincy come into the city later?" Ezekiel asked. "We could have a late lunch."

She started to shake her head.

"Come on. Pretty please?"

She yielded.

"OK."

"2?" he asked.

"2."

He leaned down and kissed her, then rose from the bed. As he left the room, Dear Heart looked over at the clock on the nightstand: 6:58. That gave her seven hours, seven hours to decide whether to unearth her secrets or try to bury them anew.

She waited until she heard the garage door open and crank back down, followed by the soft whirr of Ezekiel's car departing before she moved again. Her mind raced. When she could hear only a squirrel chuffing in a nearby tree, she reached over to the bedside table and picked up her handheld. The interview was already cued up. Dear Heart had watched Kristen Burke's network speech several times, though she hadn't seen it live. News that the heretofore-lost member of The Taken had resurfaced traveled quickly. Everyone seemed to be talking about it: all the media outlets, commentators, people in the restaurant last night. That's where she had first overheard the news and nearly choked on her paella as she struggled with the effort of chewing while hiding her shock from Ezekiel and Quincy. Like everyone else, Dear Heart thought that she would never see Kristen Burke again. After the exploitative video of her captivity was broadcast, Kristen had disappeared. Unlike everyone else, Dear Heart had last seen Kristen on the ship, tied up in the hold, breathing shallowly as Dear Heart stood over her and took her vitals one last time. Just after that, Dear Heart had escaped with TwoTone and Tailor on a lifeboat that cut through the black of a starless night.

Dear Heart had been Shireen then. But she'd left Shireen behind just as surely as Shireen had left Kristen. Now they had both resurfaced. Hearing Kristen's voice in the interview, Dear Heart could still discern the young woman who they had terrorized. Any sense of joy that Kristen had survived was enveloped in shame. Kristen had survived in spite of them and no amount of time or good deeds would change that. The past was now the present and Dear Heart could feel her life, the one she'd spent the last 15 years building, drifting away. If not today, then tomorrow, she feared — but perhaps not. Maybe there was a way to save it. First she had to get out of bed.

After another forty-five minutes, she struggled to sit up and placed both her feet squarely on the ground. Quincy banged around in his room. She should check on him, make sure that he wasn't starting any net fires or something worse.

She stood and grabbed her robe from the door.

"Q, what are you doing?" she called out as she walked into the hallway.

The door to Quincy's room swung open. Three-quarters of her height, he looked up at her.

"Nothing," he said.

He'd opened the door wide, a good sign.

"Good. Breakfast is in 30 minutes."

"OK." Quincy looked at her curiously and made a small noise in his throat, as if he were taking note of something.

She tried not to see Tailor when he looked at her that way. Today she didn't entirely succeed.

"Thirty minutes, Q." She turned back to her bedroom. She could do this. She could get through today and the next. She would follow her plans, the ones made long ago and those earlier this week: a shower first, and then the rest.

An hour later, Dear Heart dug into the dark yielding earth, emptying a hole for the new Royal Empress Tree that would shade this part of the backyard from the afternoon sun. It was early and still cool, but sweat beaded on her brow. Looking down, she watched her hands tremble as she moved them through the dirt.

Quietly, the morning news played in the background. Quincy was inside, finishing his breakfast. She plunged her spade into the ground and hit something hard. Scraping over the top of the object with the spade, she uncovered a corner of canvas fabric.

Her heart sank as soon as she saw it. Though she didn't know what it was, she knew it shouldn't be there and she had a pretty good idea who had buried it. Dear Heart looked toward the kitchen. Just don't let it be a dead something she thought and pulled the cloth until the full girth of the object was revealed: a sack. As she pulled it from the hole, an acrid smell emerged with it. She sniffed: piss. It stank of piss. With the pointed head of the spade she ripped into the canvas. The fabric separated, revealing several shiny black hard drives of Ezekiel's.

Expelling a heavy sigh, Dear Heart sank on her heels and closed her eyes.

When pressed she always said Quincy was a peculiar child. But Dear Heart knew that it was more. She was his mother after all, but she also knew the strangeness could be managed, that the good could win out. At times like this, however, her resolve wavered. Each day, he seemed to diverge more from what she hoped from him, if not entirely from what she expected.

With the sack in her hand, Dear Heart threw open the patio door and stalked into the house. The kitchen was empty; his plate sat on the counter, near the dishwasher drawer. She dropped the sack and walked to the foot of the stairs.

"Quincy! Come down here."

When he appeared at the top of the stairs, she turned and walked into the kitchen. He followed. She'd left the sack of dirty drives in the middle of the floor.

"I expect you know what this is."

She looked at him. He looked at the floor.

"You'll apologize to your father," she said.

This was Quincy's way of saying no: silently standing in front of her, gaze cut away from her and focused on the kitchen floor where the dirty sack of stolen files stank of urine and mud.

"Quincy," she said, her voice tight, "you *will* apologize to your father. This is not a discussion."

Quincy shifted his gaze to the space in front of her feet, but didn't yet meet her eyes. For him, this was a show of respect. If she had been Ezekiel or one of Quincy's teachers, he would have stared straight through her for 5, 10, 20 minutes, however long it took for the other person to grow exasperated and dismiss him.

Grounding didn't work with Quincy; punishments were born with quiet contempt; anger did not faze him. He had a single, solid scary will, much like his father, his biological father anyway. With Quincy, only Dear Heart worked, but even she couldn't stop him from doing all he did or make him regret his actions. In that way, at least he was very much like Tailor. She had always hoped he would pick up more of Ezekiel as he grew up, but the opposite seemed to be happening.

The ruined files stank. She pursed her lips and looked over at them dirtying her floor. Ezekiel had long ago stopped looking for the files. At one point, he'd even suggested that Quincy was responsible for their disappearance, but Dear Heart had defended him.

"Quincy?" Dear Heart said.

"Yes, ma'am?" he responded quietly.

"Take that sack out to the garage, clean those disks, and then go wash your hands. We're going to meet your father in the city." Ezekiel was right. It would do her some good to get back into town. They would leave early and make a day of it. She'd spent too much time here, out on the fringes.

Quincy glanced up at her, picked up the sack, and left the room. Dear Heart shook her head and gazed out the window, staring into the trees.

He was her anachronism. Dear Heart was a different person: not because she had changed her name or because the comfort of life with Ezekiel had softened her face and body. She was not the same woman on the inside. But Quincy was Shireen's child, Shireen's and Tailor's, made from the woman she was then and the man she'd met out on the edges. Quincy's devious actions showed it plainly. But Dear Heart could save him. She was not the same woman, she reminded herself, she was not, and so she could do what Shireen could not.

She no longer followed; there'd been no need after she had escaped New Dawn. That process alone had changed her. She had had to convince them she was no loose end, that nothing could tie them together. Becoming a new person had been her only option for survival. True, she had found another powerful man to love and he too had an unflagging dedication to his cause. But Ezekiel was not Tailor, and Dear Heart was not Shireen, not really. She had learned from her sins and now felt like Shireen's older relative, close enough to know her secrets, but no so close she had reason to divulge them.

Quincy and Ezekiel were her family, not Tailor and TwoTone or any of the others who'd lost themselves to a twisted vision. There were no loose ends, she reassured herself; she would not become one. This could all still work. Look here, it's working now she told herself.

A block of black in the leaves near the fence caught her attention. It seemed to hover several feet off the ground. It moved over and up. Dear Heart leaned closer to the window. She squinted, and the blur coalesced into a shape, not quite a hat, but a cap. Dear Heart froze.

She hadn't seen it in years, but she knew that cap, and the man who wore it. She knew if he took it off, his head would be two colors, the forehead a sickly pale to the chestnut face.

The perimeter alarm flashed on, a bright red across the baseboard and ceilings of the house, bathing her home in nauseating pink as it mingled with the sunlight. The cap emerged from the trees, revealing all of TwoTone and she could see him clearly. Their gazes locked. Then TwoTone took off running toward the house.

"Quincy!" she yelled. "Get down here! Now!"

A second later she heard his steps moving down the hallway.

"Now!!"

Quincy came around the corner looking perplexed and frightened. She'd never seen the look on him. Vulnerability, oddly, fit his face and made him beautiful. He looked for all the world like nothing but her baby.

A loud thud bounced off the front door.

Quincy's head snapped in the direction of the noise.

"What is that?" he asked. Dear Heart didn't answer. She threw open the cabinet doors under the sink and punched the panic button on the underside of the counter. The cool, dank air of the secret space met her hand as she searched for the pod's opening.

"What is that?" he said again, louder. She crossed the few feet between them and grabbed him by the shoulders, pulling him to the entrance under the sink. Dear Heart dropped down to one knee and stared at him, tried to drink up the soul of him in one long look. For that second, she couldn't hear the banging at the door, feel the fear in her chest, or acknowledge the rip in her world. There was only Quincy.

She kissed his forehead, placed her hand on top of his head and with the other arm shoved him into the panic pod entrance. The sound of breaking plexi reached her from the foyer.

"Love you, boy," she said and punched the button that whisked him twelve feet under the house, behind the protective layers of heat-deadening moristal where no bullet, laser, or scan could reach him.

Now alone, Dear Heart struggled to stand. They would not find her on her knees.

When TwoTone and the others broke through, both her feet were planted securely beneath her, even as her head swum at a terrible height.

Necessary Heartache

Ezekiel had almost refused to see the woman. He didn't interview potential recipients. Addie had taken on the extra responsibility and before her, it had been Dear Heart's job. Of course now she never would do it again. When Dear Heart was murdered, he had lost much more than his wife. In the five years since he found her, bled out, on the kitchen floor, every day it seemed he learned a little more of what was missing. These days, with Quincy in hiding at a boarding school under a fake name, Ezekiel had little left but his work. The thought made his headache grow, throbbing on the left side of his skull as he sat in his office, listening to the woman's voice outside his door and the protestors chanting outside the building: "Heathen Carter think you're greater than God! Heathen Carter will feel the Lord's rod!"

To make matters worse, his stomach had been iffy all day, alternating between cramps and a cloying nausea that rippled across his abdomen and down to the pits of him. He was in no shape to be the face of the equality movement right now. But even from the other side of the door, through which he could hear her pleas, the woman compelled him.

"I beg your pardon, I truly do, but if I could just speak to Dr. Carter briefly I'd leave you all in peace. I just need to talk to him for three minutes. Just three minutes," she said.

The woman had a Deep South accent and from her tone, Ezekiel didn't doubt that she'd timed what she had to say. She spoke with a calm sincerity that reminded him of his Grandma Maddie, as if she'd stand there all day until he came out or security came to remove her – and even then she'd probably just be waiting at the edge of the property to repeat herself until someone listened, found their sense, and complied.

Ezekiel opened the door before Addie could again explain that he wasn't available.

"How can I help you, ma'am?" he asked.

When the woman turned to him, her youth surprised him. Ezekiel had expected to see an older face to go along with the self-assurance he'd heard through the door. Brown-skinned with a kind face and short dreadlocks, she looked twenty or twenty-two at the most.

"Can we talk in your office?" she asked.

"Of course." He opened the door wider and swept a welcoming arm inside. He followed her in as she entered.

"Please have a seat," Ezekiel said.

She nodded and lowered herself into the chair facing his desk. Ezekiel sat on the corner of it and waited.

"Thank you for seeing me, Dr. Carter." She looked up at him and held his gaze. "I know you have your people chosen and good reasons for choosing them. But you haven't met me before. You haven't had a chance to choose me, a chance to choose my baby."

She chewed on the corner of her lip and continued.

"My name is Thelma Woods. I come from a small town in Mississippi, you probably never heard of and probably wouldn't ever want to stop in. If I weren't from there, I wouldn't either."

Ezekiel glanced down at the floor and chuckled softly. When he looked back up at Thelma Woods the mirth died in this throat.

Her steady gaze had changed in the brief seconds that he looked away. The intensity remained, but its nature had shifted.

"What I am about to tell you, I don't say for pity or for guilt. I say it 'cause it's fact. It's why we need what you have to offer. OK?" She waited for a response.

"OK," Ezekiel answered.

"I– ." she began.

Ezekiel had heard the story before, but only once: the men, the violence, the mother pleading for her daughter's innocence and the bloody, final answer to those pleas. His Grandma Maddie had told him what can happen to Black girls at the mercy of White men without any. But the ending differed. This time the girl, in this case a woman, sat before him, strong and focused if not quite whole. Still she had unearthed that memory: Grandma Maddie's long ago tale of their ancestors and the catalyst behind the bloody slave revolt that had come to define the Carters. Now the woman seemed a phantom capable of staring through his lab coat, expensive clothes, underneath and into the marrow of him where he was still soft and vital.

"What I want from you Dr. Carter is a chance, not for myself or even for the child I would carry but for my town. The Klan Riders won't stop with me, or the next girl. Back home, we need someone to protect us all – men, women, kids, young, and old. You can give us that."

"I'm terribly sorry for what happened to you Ms. Woods, but what you're asking for is something I don't do," Ezekiel replied. "I don't even know if I condone it. Here at the Center, we simply give infants a chance at a healthier life. There are organizations and specialists who sell more extreme genetic adaptations than what we offer here. Perhaps you should consult them."

"Those people aren't the best, Dr. Carter. I did my research: you are. And I *am* talking about health – for an entire community, not just one lonely old soul. You can give us that help. You can protect us."

A sudden flash of Dear Heart limp on the floor took Ezekiel's breath away. He felt his throat closing up. He stood up from the desk, and turned his back to her, facing the window. Outside the protestors stood on the other side of the barricades, gesticulating. He tried to steady himself, fingertips grazing the desktop as tears threatened to well up in his eyes. No, no, no, he thought, not now, while she's here. Slowly he breathed past the blockage and walked around the desk until he again faced Ms. Woods. As he turned back to her, he saw she was still watching him, gaze leveled on his own.

"I'm afraid you've misjudged me, Ms. Woods. I can't protect you."

She looked down at her lap and took a long breath, inhaling so deeply that her belly rounded and for a moment he could see her as she would look pregnant, could see the promise, as well as the unknown possibilities she might hold.

He tried to decipher the pang in his chest. Was that relief . . . guilt . . . resolve? Wrapped up with the day's aches and pains, he couldn't be sure. Ezekiel knew it was within his power to give her more than a disease-resistant child. He could give her a baby that fulfilled his potential as a geneticist and that might satisfy her vague hopes of protection. Or he could give her a mutation such as she could not imagine. He could do exactly the same process and have either outcome: the world was full of variables. The last five years had taught him that.

"You won't, you mean," she said.

A flash of anger burned bright and Ezekiel averted his gaze. He blinked, looking down at his hands. Was it a choice? If it was choice then he was capable of doing what she asked. Was it a choice? He chose to think it was.

Ezekiel decided to reach into the darkness and try to pull out something whole, and wholly different. The pang coalesced into an emotion more like fear. Still it was good to feel something besides discomfort or guilt. His headache dimmed.

"Perhaps I can help you after all," he said.

Her gaze found him first and then the rest of her. Her head snapped up, followed by her body as she rose from the chair to hug him, gravitating up, buoyed by his words.

Visionary

Late in the autumn, trees struggle to keep their leaves from falling to the ground already moist with their brown brethren. Ezekiel Carter, in the last hours of his life, couldn't take his eyes away from the struggle.

Technicians hurried around the lab outside of his private office, taking phenotype readings and leading the last of the expectant mothers to the armored transport vans waiting outside. Normally, Dr. Carter would be supervising every detail. Today, he reclined, feet up on his desk, intently watching a leaf spiral to the ground. As it moved past the bottom of the window, a Brown Recluse in the corner of the sill caught his eye. It walked across an ever-expanding web, working diligently to stretch the pattern ever larger. When the spider completed a broken corner, Ezekiel picked up a pen and began to write.

They call me a visionary, but I never saw it coming. I figured on a well-placed bullet or a few drops of potassium cyanide in the water supply. I never imagined the government had the patience to kill me slowly; it seemed too subtle and sentimental a means to do away with this particular Black menace. Dear Heart's assassins weren't subtle. Why should mine be? This morning's PVA confirms it: I have less than a week to complete the generation or the redressed children are just a useless human mutation with no chance of survival. And now you Quincy, like your father, must become a man too soon. So many children to raise.

I'm afraid you won't remember me from the lies they'll tell about me, even from the ones they already tell. So I'll tell you the truth now. For seven years I've struggled with the decision to send you away, but now I'm certain it was our only chance to survive, we Carters. You are the last, Quincy – though you have 127 siblings in spirit. The children will always be your family. Care for them well and they will bring joy to your life, as they have mine. God has provided for us in this way. More than ever I wish I could talk with you right now, but I'm sure they'd trace it and I can't risk you. I'll be patient and wait for you at the Center, at home.

Dad

•

Wisdom II: Respect the ancestors who made this life possible.

Quincy finished the 47th copy of the sentence with a flourish, closed the leather book and stared at the lush campus for the last time. A dozen feet away stood the two escorts his father had sent, arms crossed against their chests, dark glasses pointed at the sky.

Quincy leaned against the back of the bench, facing away from the two men. Though not quite eighteen, he cut a commanding figure in his long navy coat and stern expression. Quincy knew he wouldn't return. His gaze sought out the blue crucifix that stood beyond the academy's gates. He exhaled slowly and looked to the right, across the steeples and spires that made up downtown Glen Falls. One corner of his mouth turned up; a short burst of air shot from his nose. What would his father think of Quincy surrounded by churches? Of all the places in the world he was supposed to be safe. He chuckled into the collar of his topcoat. Of course, his father was just a man and must be forgiven this short-sightedness.

When he'd first arrived at Glen Falls Academy, Internal Protection Department posed a greater threat to then-eleven-year-old Quincy. Though biogen adaptations were common enough amongst the rich, and usually White, these were not Ezekiel's clients. More than this, his father didn't design perfect chins or quick metabolisms; he provided genetic reparations. Since the Rep War, the very use of the word 'reparations' merited surveillance and possible interrogation. One can imagine the level of alert Ezekiel must have set off: a prestigious genetics prodigy setting up an independently-funded biogen center to enhance the genetic probabilities for unborn Black babies, and later for unborn babies of any poor parents. For free. Quincy didn't imagine they had a color for that kind of alert.

Ezekiel couldn't have predicted that the congregations would turn on him. He couldn't have known that Black members of the same denominations that surrounded Glen Falls Academy would picket both the Atlanta and Louisville Centers from the day they opened – that they would decry him for drifting away from God. He hadn't foreseen their holy war. He was just a man, after all.

The wind crept up, stirring the pages of Quincy's book. He smoothed them down and closed the heavy cover. A smile spread across his face. How the congregations would froth at the mouth to know a Carter had lived amongst them for seven years in the uppity school just beyond the desiccated pond. Of course, here he was "Quincy Dorn," as he was everywhere but in his father's company. Soon, he would be someone else.

Quincy closed his eyes and breathed in the fresh air. He placed the thick leather book in the IPD grade 'sup pouch he'd bought on the net, collapsing it along its many internal spines until it was all but invisible under the long coat. He wondered how much his father surfed the net, if he knew all the things one could find there. Smiling to himself, he turned to other thoughts. Unfolding his tall frame from the bench, Quincy tried out new surnames, though he knew which one he'd claim.

The church bells began to ring. Just as the first round tones filled the sky, Quincy walked towards the two escorts.

"Mr. Zulu," one of the two said, the drably forgettable Asian counterpart to his blonde partner. The escort didn't extend his hand, but instead opened the passenger door of the sedan. "We have to make Delaware by noon, sir. Please secure your belts."

Quincy's face pinched when he heard the first two words. He hadn't yet said the name aloud and already the escort addressed him as such. With some difficulty, Quincy smoothed his expression. Looking into the escort's eyes, he absentmindedly tapped the leather book strapped to his belly.

"Sir," the escort said, "we have a tight timetable. Your belts, sir."

Quincy took a deep breath and grazed his bottom teeth across his top lip, collecting himself.

"So you already know me then? Of course." Quincy shook his head, lightly. "How could you not?"

Settling into the seat, he noted the Diplomat's ID in the dashboard and hummed a note of pleasure. They'd upgraded their cloaking tactics since his trip to upstate

New York, and rightly so. A prophet is precious cargo and worthy of every protection available.

•

Wednesday Night

You'll be here in two days. I couldn't risk a direct route and I don't think you'll mind your traveling name. I bet you thought I wouldn't remember such a small thing, but you must have watched that movie four times in two days. And you were so mad when I took it away saying you were too young. Yes, you always loved Shaka, from the first time you saw the cover art – even after I hinted at the extent of his massacres. Then I thought you stubborn and worried for you. Now I know you are a stellar student of history and your own man. Darrow Agency assures me you'll have a safe passage, and I'll have to trust them, but after seeing that movie who knows how many times I'll trust that you have remembered some of Shaka's strategies and will dispense with anything that stands in your way.

I joke, but it's been quite a day. Your old dad is tired. I'll have to tell Addie and the lab crew soon. I don't look forward to it. I made up some lie about a possible Bureau of Biological Affairs raid and that got them working quickly and carefully enough, but I can feel them looking after me as I walk back and forth, checking the insem chamber readings every five minutes. You know me. I like to take my time, but there's none left to take and there's no silence left in my head, just a list of things that must be done, and sometimes flashes of you and your mother.

Thursday 8am

Quincy, have I ever told you how much your mother loved lilac? I took a walk just after sunrise when the pains hit me. I stopped to rest under a lilac tree. All the time I was staring up at the sky, I couldn't stop looking at the cascading purple. That thought was my first poem, 'cascading purple'. She would have smiled to know now I too love them and that I'm capable of writing a poem. I wanted you to know too.

Your recent letters have meant a great deal to me. I suppose I'm trying to return the favor now. Honestly, I was afraid that you just didn't care anymore. There've always been so many tasks between you and me. Not that things have slowed down any. Still, it's been nice to hear how you're doing at Glen Falls; I had no idea you were so interested in theology, much less heading critical readings; I had to look up some of those references. Tetragrammatrons especially. But I guess history and theology go hand in hand. I must admit it's a welcome change from your minor obsession with warfare strategies. It always seemed such a curious thing for a seven-year-old to love as you did. Of course, your mother and I saw them played out on the streets. Maybe they're more fascinating in books–

Quincy, the men are here to transport the equipment. Be back soon.

●

Quincy found the noise inside the helijet soothing. Almost meditative. He retrieved his book and continued writing. The journey must be recorded so that those who came after would recognize his transition from man to more. He hoped to have the first Book completed before he reached his father. After he sent his last letter to Ezekiel he'd burned the other books. Only he should see those messy first drafts of apotheosis. He didn't want anyone skimming through the jagged lines of his pain. The pages warped with tears over Dear Heart's murder; the angry diatribes over his own invisibility within 'Quincy Dorn', the privileged son of distant parents ostensibly traveling the globe; the neat cramped capitals in which he'd written his destiny. The thought of those eyes on his naked truth made his stomach clench, so he'd burned them. And even he couldn't remember exactly what he'd said in them. Only the feeling of cold dread remained when he thought of those Books.

Flipping through the book to find his place, Quincy saw a mustard yellow corner poking out of the back pocket. Underneath the historical synopses of the riots of 2012 and '23, it lay looking at him: the envelope he had never sent to his father. Outside the sun glinted against the four inches of plexiglass between him and the clouds. A stray ray of light moved across Quincy's lap and up to his face. He closed his eyes and touched the envelope, stroked the corner. If only its contents could save Ezekiel. But soon he would see his dying father face-to-face and the world would end and begin again. It was already written. Quincy sighed and pulled the envelope from the book, tearing it into long, narrow pieces that he dropped into the trash receptacle. Quincy picked up his pen and went back to work. The helijet droned on, tearing a path through the sky.

•

Thursday 11am

A strange thought came to me while I was readying the shipment to Louisville. Do you know me? We've spent most of our lives apart.

It occurs to me now that I was naïve thinking that we would have time once the first generation was completed and I could be sure that the changes would live beyond you or me or, even beyond the history that made them necessary.

I had to do what I did, Quincy. The truth is I'm not a moving speaker. I have no patience or faith in legislation. I lived through the Rep War and knew that the government would never deliver reparations for slavery, just as I knew corporations would never compensate poor residents that lay in the path of their toxins. I had my grandmother's knowledge too and all the grandmothers' knowledge that came with her, so I did what it was in my power to do.

I'm not being clear. The strand process is completing in the lab. Everyone's asleep or gone home. The day's work is done. But this work is just starting.

It started in Alabama, during an internship at a Grey Clinic. I was never very good at recognizing the faces, but the diseases were more than familiar. They were identical to strains I'd seen in my rotations, discussed at conferences, even to those I knew were in my own family. I saw the same diseases that had killed my mother at thirty-two, then Grandma Maddie a decade later, my father and his father before him: lupus, hypertension, cardiovascular anomalies. That's when the desire was born in me: to level the playing field by getting to the origin of all this wasting and try to find a cure. I felt that I must.

I looked for colleagues, but they thought the biogen adaptations I wanted to perform were impossible. In truth, I still believe they thought them improbable. They thought I wouldn't be able to find the right alleles, master the necessary techniques, and finesse around BBA procedures, that I couldn't secure the funding to staff and equip a lab. They thought that the red tape around the African Burial Ground remains at Emory would be too daunting, but mostly that no one would support a crazy nigger like me.

They never figured on Dr. Lewis, holed up in the balmy hills of the Jamaican countryside with her money and her God complex. As she told me the day we met, "Only a crazy-brilliant nigger could mingle the DNA of the living with the dead, Ezekiel." I bristled then, but she was right. Only a crazy man would dream genetic equality so hard as to make it real. Even if it took sixteen years. If you can you must, right Quincy?

Details become a lot easier once you have a private investor. I already knew which strains I would focus on, what DNA I wanted to reintroduce, which proteins held the keys to unlock heightened health. In the beginning I thought it would only be Black people we would offer the adaptations to, but after the first three rounds, I felt no better. I realized that I was failing in the same way that Black people had been failed, by not opening up my notion of 'we' and so the Center began to invite in the poor, all the poor we could accommodate who met the other requirements. This and the work itself took up most of the last twenty years.

I can't say that I regret that, but sometimes I wish I could.

I didn't know then that that would be most of the time that I had with Dear Heart. It would have made a difference. I could have slowed down, taken time off. But Dear Heart was the last person to tell me to take a break. She believed in the work even more than I did. She believed in everything more than I did.

Your mother was the first radical that really got to me. She always hated when I called her that; she worked in an office when we met, but her opinions and the passion behind them moved me. Until then, I couldn't identify with the protestors. It hadn't yet occurred to me that you couldn't work your way past the obstacles. I didn't yet spy the yawning divide opening up between those with genetic adaptations and those without them. After Alabama, I would look back on that time and think myself a naïve child. When I met your mother, ten years my senior, she confirmed it.

From the beginning I couldn't be without her, even caught up in my own dreams of how I could bring reparations through the body. She and it were my passions, intertwined in something I still call destiny.

Dear Heart found the first volunteer. After that first child I was hooked. Your mother was too. That same day she went out to find more volunteers. "Ezekiel, you be careful and I'll be quick and we'll have reparations yet." That phrase became as routine as 'good morning', as powerful as 'I love you'.

That's why I never found anyone else to do the job. We were a team in all things, your mother and I. Of course, in time we didn't need to find volunteers anymore. They found us; unfortunately that meant all kinds of people could find us.

That day I pulled you up out of the emergency pod, I knew I couldn't keep you safe anymore. You didn't speak, wouldn't speak right up until they came to take you to Glen Falls. Then all I could say was I'm sorry. Now I can say I love you. Get here safe; get here soon.

•

They wouldn't make Nashville on time. Street barricades and radar surveillance blocked the route between the heliport rendezvous points. Though the escorts had checked navigation systems and communiqués constantly, nothing had reported the midmorning massacre that blocked their way. This was an understandable, if frustrating, limitation of technology. The government had redesigned warfare decades ago as to become invisible: no smoke, little flash fire, and total media blackout. They had no indications until they were right up on the barricades, with no way to turn back.

Quincy looked through the windshield, past the dark shoulders of the middle-aged Black couple that were his new escorts. A caravan of gray IPD trucks was parked in front. When the escorts had first shaken his hand as he exited the helijet, he wondered whether they were really a couple or just an impressive replica. The first to greet him stood a bit taller than Quincy, which had to put him at 6' 2" or above. Bundled under a topcoat and neoprene suit, Quincy couldn't guess at his actual build. This new man had the habit of looking in the extreme lower left corner of his eye before he relayed any instructions to the other man. Quincy wondered what kind of bioware he was jacked into or whether the habit was also scripted. The shorter and definitely stockier of the two men looked directly into Quincy's eyes whenever he spoke, flashing a good-humored smile. When the shorter one walked towards the waiting sedan, Quincy noticed that he led with his pivot foot, an orientation that enabled him to swing around to protect his partner as well as Quincy. Standard escort procedure dictated that one protect the client at all times. Partners were much more expendable than clients. This escort apparently thought otherwise. Though Quincy had disliked the taller man on sight, in his partner he respected the urge to protect what you love. He also noticed that the tall one did not return the favor. Perhaps this is why he reminded Quincy of his father.

Many nights Ezekiel didn't make it home to the Carters' secluded two-story outside of Roswell. To Quincy, Ezekiel merely visited. He told himself he liked it that way. All memories of missing Ezekiel were burned in Glens Falls, New York.

With them gone, Quincy could think clearly. As the embers cooled, Quincy shivered in the cold and frozen dew that defined northern nights and started the first draft of Book One. Before that night, he'd been planning to cross the Canadian border. Though he could have slipped past the border into the stream of child refugees, he did not. Why should he run or take on another identity? His mother's blood was on the Carter name. He could never forget his mother's blood.

When the men came, she protected him. Screamed his name as she never had before and he ran to her, anxiety already crawling across his face. At first Quincy thought she'd found the pictures he'd scratched out or maybe the animals. He already had a lie lodged in his throat, started to tell it. But then he heard the crash at the front door and she grabbed his shoulders, hurrying him into the kitchen. There, Quincy saw the alarm, blinking bright red across the baseboard trim. The room flashing crimson, Quincy knew the day he'd been warned about had come.

Dear Heart threw open the cabinets under the sink and punched the panic button set into the metal. She took one breath, gave her son one kiss, helped him into the pod, whispered 'love you, boy', and then was gone.

In the last seven years, he'd imagined three notebooks of scenarios: exactly how his mother had died after the dark enveloped him (he envisioned many of these waiting for his father to respond to the wrist com wired between him and the panic button); how he could have saved her; and why Ezekiel was incapable of doing so. Before he began the Books, Quincy couldn't understand why a biogenetic genius didn't have a better plan for his family. Now he knew he must respect his father's limitations, as well as the life he'd made possible. Ezekiel, after all, gave the prophet a people and a means to make his miracle come true.

"Mr. Zulu."

Quincy jolted, turned his head from the trucks and met the escort's gaze. "We'll have to divert to Detroit and connect you from there."

"Fine," he answered, "just get me there."

•

Friday 12:17am

Quincy, we've finished the last procedures. Everyone's gone home. I believe we've diversified enough, and the adaptations will survive this generation. As of now, this Center is closed. The others will close in the coming year, with enough time to fulfill scheduled procedures and for the staff to find new positions. The Louisville Center will become a closed archive. I've sent some of the family things, as well backups of my work. It's strange to see your life's work turn into artifacts. Addie will take care of all the details. I know it's the last thing you want to deal with.

After all these years, my work is done.

I think you can be Quincy Carter again; with me and the Centers gone, there's no real reason to hide, though I would suggest you try something out of the States. You could finish your schooling in Costa Rica or New Zealand; they have some wonderful programs. There's a whole world out there. I wish I could see what you'll do in it.

•

Quincy walked through Nashville in long strides. He imagined himself draped in black and crimson robes, nodding to well-wishers lined along his path. He tilted his head back with the weight of a headdress that was not there. The men and women on the street paid him no mind. His escorts, two steps behind, subtly cased the crowd. Quincy looked up at the towering Two Rivers Baptist, one of the few mega-churches to survive the Rep War. His eyes saw it filled with thousands of Carter Kids serving the purpose, beaming out Quincy's scriptures to thousands more. He smiled a secret smile, corners of his mouth turned up a centimeter.

One day it would be his. There must be at least a few dozen Carter Kids in the city and surrounding counties. By the time he branched out, a congregation would be waiting for him, eager to serve the Prophet Father. The other churches would cower before his miracle. In competition for souls, nothing trumps a messiah. And Quincy meant to make one.

By the time they reached the rendezvous and then the heliport, Quincy's spine buzzed with anticipation. He secured his belts and took out Book One of the Church of the Evolved Spirit, started writing before the wheels left the ground.

•

Friday 5:24:41 am

IPD assassins are not only subtle; they have a shitty sense of humor. After I told the team what was going on, Addie insisted on a diagnosis. I knew the virulence levels were too high to arrest progress, but I acquiesced. She just told me the results. It's a VDV. A Fucking VDV!

Do you remember when we opened the other Centers? I got the money from leasing out rights to the Madolin Process, the one that affects rheumatoid arthritis and Sjorgen's Syndrome? Anyway the boys from the Bureau of Biological Affairs were impressed. They approached me about creating an entron virus. I called it a voo doo virus because it worked along the same lines of the doll. You needed a person's DNA sample (a lock of hair, a piece of nail). With it, you could activate all their unexpressed phenotypes and send the system haywire. Like anthrax with a homing signal. Of course, I refused. The bastards went ahead with it and stuff a lot nastier than that. Addie tells me you can even find formulas and replicating contractors on the net! Unfortunately the antidote takes weeks to synthesize and has to be applied through the same medium. We still have no idea how it was transmitted to me. So I'm back where I started, but at least I got a good laugh out of it. And the way the pains have been hitting me I could use a good laugh.

●

Ezekiel could no longer speak to the Brown Recluse that had kept him company in the hours between dark and dawn. His voice had given out, windpipe viced between the swollen glands that distorted his once-graceful neck. He contented himself with watching the spider spin its web while he waited on his son to come home.

Ezekiel almost didn't hear Quincy open the door, or have the strength to rise from his chair. When he saw his son, his hands shook with excitement, eyes wide with delight. He could see Quincy reflected in the window, now taller than Ezekiel. Could see the curve of Dear Heart's muscle in his arms and broad shoulders. Quincy's face was blurred in the web. Ezekiel turned to look at him.

And stopped at the eyes: pinning him down, from a distance. Ezekiel blinked.

Quincy smirked, walked towards his father, sat down in the guest chair, and waited for him to die.

An hour later – still sitting at his desk, knees pulled into his chest, shivering against the cold inside him and that radiating from his only child – he did. Just before his heart stopped, his arms flailed up, catching the edge of the window. The web, now broken, drifted slowly towards Ezekiel's face, brushed past his closed lids and settled on his lips.

Soft Spot

Quincy had birthed a religion and surely that must have made him a god, omniscient. The logic was infallible and his calculations of grandeur, his taxonomy of the soul flawless. Why then did he find himself in this situation? A test, he realized, of course a test.

Quincy crumpled the letter and threw it to the other side of the room. Fine, he wouldn't have access to the old fool's genetic records. He wouldn't need them. In deference to his vision, the world had cracked open with possibilities. He didn't need his dead father's genetic records or his expertise; He had the free market.

Biogenetic adaptations were readily available for whoever had the money and Ezekiel had left him plenty of that. Quincy would have his messiah. He would find his apostles and they would find his believers, and if one of them would not birth his messiah then one of them could become his messiah – or at least as much as was necessary for people to believe in the god who had made Him, or perhaps Her, he thought amused. Yes that might be it exactly, a competitive edge. Believers would elevate his glory to undeniability. He stood in the atrium of his new building, which would soon be the first Church of the Evolved Spirit and savored the clarity of his conviction.

The next day Quincy signed the last of the paperwork for the building. A week later, workmen installed the closed circuit surveillance system inside his private chambers. The pews, altar and throne were delivered ten days later and as it turned out, Quincy had to hire his apostles.

In the dim glow of the closed circuit screens a few feet from his bed, he watched as they herded the first of his flock. This setup was not quite up-on-high or omniscient as he had imagined, but at this proximity at least he could see the details of their mortal lives. And what he couldn't see, he already knew. The apostles were merely his hands, out in the world working his will.

•

In the alley behind an empty building, deep in the District, Ach Devonshire sat at a makeshift table with Curt the Cunt and some wannabe card shark asshole. Ach fingered the divine hand that would make him 140 cred richer.

The card shark's name was Darnell Bailey. And aside from this immaterial piece of information, Darnell knew a few more things that Ach didn't. He knew a mess of spades wouldn't beat a White House, and he was still figuring on how to trick his way lucky before his partner came outside to collect. He kept up conversation, trying to steal their eyes from his hands and into his albino face. It was an old trick, but he hoped it would hold until he could do a new one: maybe hide a card between the wrist ports that kept him jacked into the surveillance cameras bolted behind the two men or, even easier, activate the holo patches on the corner of each card until he had a better hand.

Across the alley, the building door swung open. A path of light cut across the littered ground, carved its edges onto the far wall. Darnell and the marks turned toward the sudden intrusion. They weren't worried about cops. Darnell had picked this place special; no cops came around here. Like most everyone else, they were scared of this part of town. Darnell wasn't scared a' nothing, for true. Claiming a territory in an alley on the darkest corner of the District proved he was a bad sum'bitch, something Darnell liked to prove.

Out stepped a figure from the blind-bright doorway. It brushed the door closed and stood staring in the direction of the three men.

"Ach, maybe we ought to call it a night," the mark across from Darnell said to his companion. His eyes darted back and forth between Ach and Darnell, careful not to look at the figure by the building door.

Darnell quickly tapped the upper right hand corner of the spades in his hand and confirmed, on his eyes' second pass that he now held two queens, a king and a pair of other spades: a For True Family that only a Hand of Rage could beat.

Ach, a chunky dropping of a man, turned to the other mark. The phospho beams lit up his gray whiskers as he spoke.

"You still afraid of the boogey man, Curt? We ain't going nowhere till we finish this hand." His eyes darted down to the White House folded into his doughy hand. "You don't leave a game in the middle of a hand. Or didn't your bitch of a mammy teach you that?"

Curt's chest ached at the harsh words. After 27 years it still found a way to ache, the same way Ach always gave Curt's yellowing bruises a new coat of purple when the mood struck him. Things never got a chance to heal around Achilles. Wounded, Curt's head shrunk down in his shoulders. The figure leaned against the door, body squared toward the group of men.

Darnell didn't speak on it one way or the other. He kept his expression neutral as the Rep War was long. He'd already made a week's worth of expenses on the two and could take or leave this hand. But he wanted to take it just the same.

The sound of footsteps cut the marks' argument short. The figure, draped in white, stepped into the line of the phospho beams, and moved toward them. From the curves, it was clearly a woman; he wondered if the marks had caught on. Her eyes lit up a moment, reflective as a cat. Darnell felt dirty business coming on, relished the rush. He drummed his fingers on his knees and sent the wrist ports four millimeters deeper into his skin, nestling into the space between his veins. Hissing a bit at the pain, he looked at the woman coming toward him.

She stopped a few feet in front of the men and looked over their heads towards the mouth of the alley. Darnell glanced in the same direction, while the others stared at the woman wrapped in white. Only her honey-colored face and long hands were visible beneath the lengths of cloth.

Curt flinched when saw her hands; they ended in abbreviated talons. The eyes could have been contacts, though a bit expensive for a woman alone in the District, but the claws proved she was Adapted. He'd never been so close to an Adap. In his world, only the rich went in for the cosmetic wings, cat eyes, and clit patches that defined Adaps to Curt. Of course, he'd gotten most of his information from the 'bloid net; but still they never said anything about normal people having them, much less women walking out of abandoned buildings situated in Atlanta's worst neighborhood. In his neighborhood, Reynoldstown, he knew no one could afford the costly procedures. She was otherwise, quite beautiful.

The marks waited for her to speak or move, or otherwise release them from their dumb-dumb spell. Darnell spoke instead.

"Evening. Taking a break from the services?" he asked.

Dragging her eyes from further down the alley, she crooked her head at him, a smile playing at her lips.

"No services tonight," her voice was deep and relaxed, "just a joining." She inhaled deeply, eyes almost closing. "I thought there might be someone out here." She chanced another glance into the dark and turned her head back to the men. "And here you are."

The marks looked behind them past the garbage cans and saw nothing. She stepped closer and crouched at the edge of Darnell's case near the makeshift table. Ach and Curt tensed.

"Deal me in," she said.

Darnell spoke when the others obviously couldn't.

"We're in the middle of a hand," he said.

She smirked, staring at the spot where his ports had descended into skin. Looking at the others, she nodded and settled farther back in the air. Some color returned to Ach's pallid face as he fanned his cards out in his hands.

"I call," the large man said, already turning his cards over. His features flared in triumph. "And I win."

Curt cursed under his breath and threw in his paltry hand.

Darnell clucked his tongue and stopped Ach's smile, laying out the For True Family, ladies in, flanked by the warrior hologram on both sides.

"Son of a pig fucker!" Ach exploded. He caught sight of the woman in white at his side and settled a bit.

Darnell played it cool, swept his cards sheepishly to the side, and wanded Curt's authorization code, hesitating at the fuming Ach.

"Settle?" he said all polite smiles and empathetic eyes. Though his tone was benign, they both knew about the gun in his coat, just as Darnell had looked over the pistol holstered near Ach's ankle: gentleman's rules.

"You already got me for 150 cred. No way I'm giving up 90 more," Ach said.

Darnell dropped the ruse and spoke straight.

"Listen up, fat man. You raised when your buddy folded. You dug this hole. Now give me my due or I'll take it out of your ass." He drummed his fingers across the tabletop and nodded to the other mark. Darnell bluffed.

"You're settled. Time to get home," Darnell said to the smaller man.

Curt turned toward Ach, not really wanting to leave him in such company. The Adap caught his eyes first. Unaccustomed to a beautiful woman's gaze, much less an Adapted one, Curt quickly stood and started to walk down the alley without a second glance at his companion.

"You fucking humper! Where do you think you're going?" Ach yelled at his back.

Curt turned. "Just pay him," he said, though he knew Ach wouldn't. Curt took another step towards the street and then hesitated. Nervous as the woman made him, it was difficult to resist the chance to watch his tormentor tormented, to see Ach down, maybe even see him cry. He looked out into the street; the scent of ozone hung in the air. Best to get home before he had to brave the District alone under dark clouds. But the street was empty. Curt decided to fool bravery and stay. He stepped into half-shadow and waited for the asskicking to commence. Anxious, he turned his attention back to Ach.

The big man held the pistol pointed at the ground, glaring at the grifter. He unloaded a litany of expletives that only succeeded in reddening his skin. Darnell felt relaxed, more than a little amused. He leaned back in his chair, tipping the front legs into the air. He glanced at the woman in white. She rested her head on a loose fist, talons hanging under her chin. Her eyebrows shot up at particularly colorful passages.

After three or four minutes, Darnell had chuckled all he cared to.

"You want your money back, you win it back," he said, looking steadily at the quivering mound of a man. "You lose, you pay what I say."

The woman cracked a smile and stood up to her full height.

Ach wasn't beyond realizing that she had moved a step closer to him. He almost brought the barrel up, but then thought of Curt telling the crew he'd leveled on a woman. Underground crews had a pecking order. They didn't care that women had fought and commanded in the Rep War or that women held the flyweight and bantamweight belts. If he leveled on her, he was as good as Curt underground – no kind of good at all. In that light, survival instinct flared and faded. He holstered the gun at his waist.

"I pick the game," Ach said. Spittle flew from his lips on the 'p'. "And we use my deck."

"You have your own deck?" Darnell said, resting the chair on the asphalt. "My, my, my. You must be a regular player."

"Regular enough." Ach shifted uncomfortably, eyed the woman, and tossed a glance at the alley's shadows. Ach pulled the deck from his jacket and slid it over for Darnell's inspection. Darnell turned the deck face up, spread the cards across the case, and flipped them back over.

"And the name of the game?" Darnell asked.

"Dark Sky," Ach answered slowly.

Decades ago someone had decided that Russian Roulette was for candy asses – that person invented Dark

Sky. You didn't play for your life, but for what it meant to you. In choosing this game, Ach revealed that 240 credits was life to him. Through idle District conversation, Darnell already knew the welder owed more than ten times this amount to bookies around the District – the same bookies that had put a lien on Ach's glands, causing him to gain 100 lbs. in four months and given him a special hunger for cred. Ach was betting to win and Darnell knew that too. He shook his head and tried not to snicker at the big man.

In the alley's shadows Curt came a few steps closer, improving his angle.

The woman in white spoke. "I will be your Watcher."

Ach gulped though he knew it inevitable. The stranger was chancy, but the only option. Dark Sky needed a third and he'd trust her over Curt. After twenty years of trying to beat, cajole, and shame him into a man, Curt was still a hopeless little sniveler, Ach thought. Yeah, he'd take the freak over his friend. The Watcher in the Dark Sky was in no physical or financial danger so he thought she'd keep her claws to herself.

In this decision Ach though not entirely ignorant, was a touch stupid. If one were kind, it could be said that he didn't know enough to be sufficiently afraid.

He played his hand.

If Darnell were a normal man, Ach would have won. The big man would have emptied Darnell's accounts, and taken all the gear hidden in and outside of his body. Ach had a skill for the complex game and could have won all the things written on the lists that the Watcher held in her hands. But Ach never saw the list because he played a bad sum'bitch and so he did not win.

Now he waited to see what the grifter would leave him, if anything. Darnell folded the small list into his palm and motioned for Ach's authorization code to transfer the funds. Clenching his jaw, the big man handed it over. He stared at the wall so hard he almost didn't notice the balance when Darnell was finished: 240 credits. A muscle above his right cheek twitched as he looked up at the albino shining in a stray beam of light.

"You lose, you pay what I say," Darnell repeated.

"That's all I have," Ach said.

"It's not yours to give. You already owe it," Darnell answered.

Ach's mind inventoried what else he could spare. One kidney already did the work of two; he'd traded his spleen for 4000 cred; there wasn't much of a market for fingers and he needed those for his work. While his mind calculated, his body began to twitch and tense, anticipating another loss. Across from him, Darnell read him expertly.

"I don't want your guts, big man," Darnell said as the woman in white moved into the shadows. "I want your pride."

Ach's face tensed. "My what?"

Darnell didn't answer at first, only stared into the shadows, waiting.

"Seems you've stolen some. And that you have. That you owe."

Curt stepped into the light, the woman in white whispering in his ear. Her words were swift and soft, intuiting the history of Ach Devonshire and Curtis Baker – the unkind deeds, the shitty words, Curt's shunted thoughts of escape. Stroking decades of hurt, she conjured up the soft spot where she and Darnell would strike: Curt's heel, Achilles.

"You weren't so kind to your friend there," Darnell said, still seated at the makeshift table. "Haven't been for a long time, it seems."

"Fuck him. What's this got to do with him?" Ach answered, the red returning to his face. He pressed his palms into his knees and slowly stood. Curt and his new companion came closer, the smaller man's eyes fixed on Ach. The woman in white leaned, hands clasped behind her back, into Curt, still whispering.

Darnell re-decked his wrist ports, pressed his thumb just to the left of a bright blue vein and switched the relay. Ach eyed him suspiciously, came closer to the table.

"What the fuck are you doing?" he spat.

Darnell glanced up as he picked up his case, unlocked and opened it. Cards fell to the ground.

"Preparing to take my due."

Darnell unlatched a clasp and a small motherboard slowly dropped down to his waiting fingers. Two codes later and he completed the transfer. He damped the signal and waited, his face glowing bright in the screen's light.

Darnell, the bad sum'bitch, almost missed it. If it weren't for the way Ach's eyes swelled, he would have missed seeing the first blow. Darnell stowed the keyboard just as Curt, sweating and mewling, knocked two teeth out of Ach's head. The big man wasted time reaching for a pistol that he'd given to the Watcher before the game started. He paid for his forgetfulness with a sharp jab to his ribs. He howled and stumbled into the far wall.

"You little shit!" Ach screamed. "I'll fucking kill you!" He held his side and lunged for the smaller man.

Curt backhanded him, leaving a bright red welt on Ach's cheek. The bully held his face, blinked. Sweat rolled down his chin.

"Curt, it weren't my fault!" Ach wheezed.

Curt slapped him twice more, punched him in the chest, stood back and glared at him.

Ach, now doubled over, started to slide down the wall, gathered enough breath to speak again.

"She gave it to me. Never asked her," he choked out.

"Liar!" Curt yelled.

"It's true," Ach answered, his breath coming back to him.

Curt's fists loosened. He took a step back, thinking. Her face had been soft when he caught them fumbling against each other in her dusty bedroom. Had she given Ach the money? Did her voice have the lilt of lying when she told him where the 800 cred had gone? Curt couldn't remember anything past the sight of his 73-year-old mother perched on top of Ach's sweaty pale body, the tips of her wrinkled breasts sliding across his bulbous stomach. Doubt touched Curt and he felt a whisper of warmth for the man he'd known so long. It blasted to red-hot rage when Ach spoke again.

"She gave it to me 'cause I gave it to her *good*." Ach smiled around the new holes in his mouth. He could see he was dealing with good old asshole Curt again.

Curt stood frozen, his shirttail flapping in a tender breeze. He thought of kicking in Ach's face, but decided against it. Better to tip his bookies to the hard currency stashed in the old switch boxes under Alta Avenue, let Ach's own trespasses be what finally closed the book on him. Curt backed away, spitting on the ground inches from Ach's head.

While Ach figured out the odds of living this down, Darnell and the woman in white ushered Curt into the back door of the building.

•

"You chose well," the Prophet Father said. He emerged from His private chambers and entered the back room where the novice stood between the apostles. He approached His first initiate and smiled at him warmly, favoring him with a touch on the shoulder. It was the same height as His own; His arm felt like a bridge between them, solid and level. The initiate was a lucky young man, the Prophet Father thought. He smiled at the gifts the boy would receive. Why the Prophet Father had written two new wisdoms just watching the scene play out in the alley. The boy reminded Him of Himself, or what He had once been, a bit like a cloudy mirror in which Quincy's apotheosis was well reflected. Again, creation had deferred to Him.

"You did choose well," Darnell said, turning to the woman in white. "He looks just like him."

"Of course he does," she responded.

Darnell's arm shot out. The Prophet Father saw only a blur at first, then clearly the short length of steel pipe just before it cracked into the side of His skull. His head snapped to the side and legs gave out as he crumpled to the floor.

For who knew how long – his mind stuttered on the thought he could not know how long – he could hear nothing. Sound came back to him suddenly as he blinked down at the floor where his blood had begun to pool.

"Did you finish with his accounts?" the woman in white asked.

"Empty," Darnell responded.

"Good. I already picked up the lenses and print gloves so I'll take Curt with me for the face-to-faces tomorrow. As for this one, just tie him up, preferably to his precious chair in there," she said snickering.

Quincy felt arms hoist him up and the dig of a sharp bone in his gut as he was thrown over someone's shoulder. His shoes scraped along the ground. This indignity would not stand! As they moved through the threshold and back into the hallway that led to his private chambers, he opened his mouth to decree and saw a pair of hips move under him, snapping quickly to the left. He felt his head make contact with the side of the door and the world bled away.

Quincy woke on his throne, nauseous. A horrendous pain threatened to split his head in two. Dull sunlight crept through the room. In his lap sat the morning mail. They had tied him loosely, as if unworried about his eventual escape, and he pulled his hands free with ease. To his bones, he felt ravaged, less than mortal. How far and quickly the sublime one had– fuck he couldn't even think straight.

He let his head drop back and stared at the ceiling. When he opened his eyes, the envelope on the top of the pile caught his attention. On it his name, his full legal name, was written in sweeping cursive hand. He opened it and read.

Quincy,

I thought it only fitting that I write you this letter – because I know what you did.

Ezekiel was so sure it was the government. But with the protestors and corporate competition I had my doubts even with the security measures we've taken. I'm glad he never knew it was his only son – a son who he loved more than I now know you are capable of understanding. Best also that Dear Heart will never know either.

You can't hide; the same gene trace that your parents had implanted to ensure your protection makes it impossible. As executor, I've frozen all of your remaining assets. I've also alerted the authorities and supplied them with proof of your crime. A just man should have justice. And this is what you should have.

Addie

Live Forevers

Even war couldn't take away the dew. The early morning sun glinted through the haze and lit up the scattered fields as the Woods' drove slowly through what was left of Erlanger, Kentucky. Jesse and William shared the backseat, while Raynard rode shotgun with Mama. The boys stared through the window, pointing at the scintillating grass, seeming just boys for a moment. Mama stole looks at Raynard and into the rear view mirror at her two other sons. She almost held her breath, not wanting to break the moment.

There was no dew left in Mound Bayou, just dirty smears of sooty condensation. Mississippi hadn't been a particularly pretty place since the Riders came back: broken windows, charred remnants of fool's crosses, misspelled hatred spewed on sidewalks and once-stately trees. But after the Klan Riders started burning the outposts and little towns that surrounded Mound Bayou, Thelma couldn't sweep the soot quickly enough to keep the porch from looking like a split coffin, freshly unearthed. She didn't want to sweep; out in the open air she could feel her neighbors' eyes piercing through her and into her home. She could feel those eyes searching past her, looking for her boys. They smiled alright – Miss Eunice, Brother Jerry and the rest. They gave Thelma tight smiles that said, 'You best to enjoy it; time's almost up.'

Before Thelma gave her precious triplets to the town that had helped pay their way, she brought them here, to the place that had created them just as surely as she had: Dr. Ezekiel Carter's hometown. Though Thelma knew Dr. Carter was long laid in the ground, she also knew a place could make a person; just as surely as Mound Bayou had made her and her boys, yes indeed. Things being as they were, Thelma almost couldn't blame her community. But today, listening to her boys' chatter and take in the green, she could blame them to hell and back. A dash of bitter emerged on her young face, tightening the wrinkles around her eyes into crow's feet.

Raynard reached out and touched the steering wheel, close to the hand that gripped it. He looked up at her and began to speak. William cut him off with a shout of delight.

"Mama! Look!" the eleven-year-old's huge hand shot through the narrow space between Thelma's seat and the window. He cranked her window down and pressed his forehead to the headrest, hovering close to her ear.

"Rainbow," William whispered, voice deeper than her daddy's.

Wet air rolled into the car, filling it with the smell of grass and damp earth. Sure enough a hundred yards off to the right, a faint rainbow shimmered in the morning mist. It stretched across half a fallow field. Just as Thelma started to slow the car down, the sun rose higher and burned the rainbow into invisibility. The boys sighed quietly. Before Thelma could comfort them with the promise of more rainbows, she saw the smiles on their faces, caught the contentment in that sigh. She shook her head slightly and gave their smile back to them. Her chest tightened as she looked at them – Raynard's deep dimples, William's bright eyes, Jesse's high cheekbones already sprouting stubble – but she smiled.

This trip was her gift to them. The boys had never been out of Mississippi and sometimes Thelma forgot she ever had; though the boys themselves were proof of her sole excursion out of Mound Bayou.

Everyone in town had heard about the clinics where you could plan your children, not just when or how, but who. Most folks rolled their eyes or shook their heads when they heard; many took to praying. They called it trifling city business sure to bring damnation. And couldn't Black folks think of something better to do with their money? Build a school? Or a community center? Fund a church? Anything had to be better than designing babies.

Thelma had heard it all reshelving the books in the library. One thing about folks in Mound Bayou: they loved to come to the library for their conversations. They didn't have to buy anything to spend a few hours and with most of the community businesses put out of business by the conglomerates in Sunflower County, free space was a precious thing. And though they probably wouldn't even admit it to themselves, folks didn't like to be outside too much.

Especially after the Riders started stringing up boys in Winstonville. Then Fred Hoss found the Charles girl dangling from a sycamore. She was the first of four that the sheriff declared a suicide. Hate crimes didn't exist anymore 'cause things was so equalized now what with everyone having the right to die in undeclared wars right here on American soil. So no FBI. They were busy investigating racial skirmishes all around the state; apparently there were just too many Black folks to kill in Mississippi and Mound Bayou hardly left a mark on the map.

After all the petitions and marches fell short; after all the activists went on to the next disaster site; after the natives failed night after night to keep their property and families safe and the hired security moved on to more lucrative jobs, the folks in Mound Bayou started to change their minds about the whole clinic thing. They started to think they needed someone who was invested in the town as they were – someone who would want to keep it safe for future generations, as they did. So while they kept up with short-term tactics, they collected pennies from their purses, tucked away the extra dollar from grocery change and started discussing biogenetics over card games and dinner rolls.

At first they didn't understand they couldn't just send off for some protectors. Thelma was the first to truly realize that they would be babies. And that someone would have to birth those babies. Would have to potty train them, draw out their bee stings with detergent, give them their first taste of strawberry, and then send them out into the night to face the Klan.

"Mama, I'm hungry," Jesse said from the backseat. He pulled at a thread in his jeans, long legs folded under and around the lip of the seat. Next to him, William, head pressed against the roof, chimed in.

"Yeah, Mama can we eat soon?" he asked.

She looked at Raynard, "You hungry, too?" she asked.

"Yes, Ma'am" he replied. A sly smile crossed his mouth.

"Mama?" Raynard said.

She brushed thick locks from her chestnut face and glanced at him.

"Can I drive?" he asked.

"No, boy," she waved her right hand and set her eyes back on the road.

"But Mama, Ches and Oday are already driving and they're four months younger than us," he said.

Thelma knew that. A lot of the children in Mound Bayou drove – cars, buses, even the few solar tractors left in one piece. She herself had learned to drive at thirteen, just before her Grandmama took to the big mahogany bed and never got back out. Thelma, pressed and greased, had driven her and her father to the funeral in her grandmother's prized Masquerade hybrid, shined just as bright as Thelma for the occasion. She led her father to the gravesite and wiped the tears from his blind eyes. All within the first month of learning how to drive.

"Well I ain't Oday and Ches's mama, now am I?" she answered. Raynard nodded, kept smiling.

They drove past piles of weathered wood planks pulping in the moisture, the last remnants of abandoned farmhouses. Old machinery rusted into sculptures beside them. Thelma wondered if Mound Bayou would look that discarded in another twenty years. With the fires, there wouldn't be anything left, she concluded. Her boys were supposed to prevent that future. Her stomach tightened. No cars passed them on the road.

"We'll eat at the Carter home," she said, shifting in the cloth seat, "should be another twenty-five miles or so."

Raynard and William sat quietly, staring out the windows; Jesse stroked his chin. Her boys didn't fidget, never had, like they'd injected some calm with all those alleles and proteins. Of course, warriors probably wouldn't fidget, she thought. Don't fidget, she corrected herself. She didn't have to guess what the boys would be like anymore; they were right here with her. Still, she sometimes caught herself doing it, an old habit.

On the trip to Georgia, Thelma had exhausted her mind. After she'd spent months learning about phenotypes, behavioral genetics, and biogenetic adaptation; going through net portals and public records

119

scouring for any mention of the Carter Center; and convincing the community council and her father that she could do it and should be the one, there was nothing left to do in the high perch of that rickety transport semi but wonder what it would feel like to carry such a baby inside her and who she would meet when it was done.

She'd already named the baby Billy Ray, after her father. When the doctors told her she'd have triplets, Thelma split the name between them and named the last after the nurse, Jessenia, who held her hand and sang "Duerme de mi Niña" while they peeled Thelma back like an overripe fruit and wrestled the boys out. The doctor guffawed at their size. Thelma wasn't surprised; her legs hadn't had the strength to lift her after the second trimester.

At eleven, the boys already had to look down at her 5'3" frame. Thelma pulled over to the road's soft shoulder, parked next to a field bordered by tall grass and a dense row of pink and yellow flowers.

"Y'all wanna stretch your legs?" she asked.

The doors were open before she finished the question. She killed the engine and joined the boys. Outside it was cool and moist, the sun losing its fight to dodge the clouds. Thelma didn't mind; she relished having to pull her sweater closer to her shoulders as she hitched one leg up and leaned against the hood. She watched as Jesse walked towards the high grass that sprouted a few feet from the road. William walked farther down, and Raynard up, before they too moved into the brush. Their eyes scanned back and forth, knees bent slightly. Thelma didn't think the boys realized that they walked in formation, that they always had. When the Woods walked through town, Billy and Ray flanked her sides, Jesse bringing up the rear. When she'd realized what they were doing she'd tried to break them from the habit. It lasted all of three days. She couldn't stand to see them cast their eyes everywhere, breathing unevenly, losing the rhythm of their own steps. Right there next to the First Federal she told them to forget what she'd said and they floated back to their positions, like magnets in easy alignment, she their precious center. She'd never again tried to suppress their instincts.

Even last week when she'd come across William's smoke-stinking clothes soaking in the basin behind the house. She stood there staring down at the gray-pink water, the freckles of blood on the cuff that floated above the surface. For how long she didn't know.

Today William wore the cranberry button-down the girl had brought him. It stretched across his chest as he turned to wave at Thelma, motioned for her come join them. All clear, she thought, as she lifted her foot from the bumper and walked towards the tall grass.

William had had enough sense not to tell Thelma what happened. But the news came quickly enough. Not two hours after she'd found the clothes Ms. Johnson's granddaughter, Eileen, stood at her door with a plate of fresh rolls and a side of ham from the hog her family had butchered a month ago. No one had brought Thelma anything as precious as ham since she'd finished nursing the boys. She looked at the girl cautiously. In the afternoon light, Thelma could see the shadow of a bruise forming under one eye, caught the same sooty smell from the girl's hair and knew this food was for something William had saved her from. Thelma didn't even want to know that much, but held no malice towards the child and so took the food gently and started to thank her for her family's kindness when Old Ms. Johnson interrupted the gratitude with the steady knock of her cane up the wooden steps.

Eileen moved to the side and took her grandmother's elbow as the older woman reached the doorway. In old age, Mae Johnson had started to look like a walnut, brown, creased, and round. Only the cane and her aqua floral dresses proved she hadn't completely crossed over into this new incarnation.

"Afternoon, Thelma," she said, smiling.

"Afternoon, Ms. Johnson," Thelma answered. Courtesy said Thelma should invite her in, but she didn't want that story coming in with her so she hesitated. In that second the old woman turned to her granddaughter.

"Eileen, wait for me," she said. Her gaze pointed at the stand of trees next to the front steps.

With a "yes, ma'am" Thelma and Ms. Johnson stood alone on the porch in the hazy afternoon light. Flecks of ash danced around their faces; One or two settled on Ms. Johnson's plaits, got lost in the white.

"Thelma Ann," Ms. Johnson said, looking up at her, "peace of mind is *precious*." The weight on the last word made Thelma study Ms. Johnson's face. She squinted at the old woman. Who was she to tell Thelma her duty when Ms. Johnson had no idea what it felt like to be Raynard, Jesse and William's mother? Brought into this world to restore the community's peace of mind, the specter of her boys' fate had left Thelma awake at night and sleepwalking through the day, always wondering 'when'?

Ms. Johnson rapped her cane loudly on the floor.

"Those boys, those *Riders*, they almost stole Eileen's peace of mind." Ms. Johnson's voice started to tremble, then settled in its depths.

Thelma's eyebrows tensed. She stopped anticipating the words and heard them.

"I told her to leave the salvaging to the men. Merigold ain't no place for her, especially at night. Her and that Thompkins Boy went. Didn't even wait till the fire died out. That Thompkins ran off, left her to 'em. Billy" – she looked over at her sixteen-year-old granddaughter, caught the girl's full eyes for a moment, then swung her head back to Thelma's – "saved her peace of mind."

•

Out beyond the high grass the boys were being themselves: Jesse tumbling through somersaults and back handsprings, a soft whoosh of air punctuating each exertion; Raynard peering intently at a goldenrod; William sitting in the bough of an oak tree, big feet dangling down.

"Mama," William called down. She looked up through the branches, sweeping a dreadlock from her face.

"Can we eat here?" he asked. He looked back out across the land. "I don't see nothin' for miles."

"Y'all that hungry?" she asked.

"Yeah!" Jesse and Raynard said.

She didn't know if it was safe to eat here right next to the road. They hadn't see another car once they got off the highway and state troopers were underfunded right out of existence years ago, but still . . .

William spoke up.

"It'll be alright, Mama." He glanced at his brothers and they nodded in assent.

Her lips pursed. The boys gazed calmly back. "Alright then."

Jesse ran past her to the car. The youngest by twelve minutes, Jesse was smaller than his brothers and, as they all knew, considerably faster – faster than anyone Thelma had ever known. If the middle school or even Kennedy Memorial was still open, Thelma knew her baby would be a track star. As it was, she enjoyed watching him run almost as much as he seemed to enjoy the chance to unfurl those long, sinewy legs and get gone. She walked over to Raynard and rested her hand against his wide back.

"What you got there?" Thelma asked.

"Solidago virgauria." He brushed his thick finger against the cluster of small yellow flowers. "Don't see many down home."

"Hey, Ray," William called. "What are those?"

He pointed to the dense outcropping of pink and yellow blossoms that covered the land twenty feet beyond the oak tree. From this distance Thelma could see the flowers sprouted at least an acre or two further into the field. Nothing else grew around them, even grass.

"I don't know," Raynard answered. He began to walk to the flowers.

Jesse returned with the big insulated sack of food and an old blanket.

"Right here, Mama?" he asked.

"No," she answered, "let's eat over there." She pointed at the spot Raynard moved toward. William jumped the fifteen feet from his perch, landed on his feet with a soft thud. Jesse handed him the sack of food and pulled up the rear.

Raynard seemed to have forgotten all about the food. His gaze scanned the river of blossoms, resting for a moment on the stout light green stems, then the large thick leaves growing in bushels. Up close, they could see white blossoms mixed in with the pink and yellow, floating three feet above the ground. Raynard reached out to touch a leaf.

"Careful," Thelma warned, "they're sticky."

He stroked the leaf delicately between his thumb and middle finger. Releasing it, he rubbed his fingers together, felt the gummy residue.

"What are they?" William asked again.

"Live Forevers," Thelma said. She took the blanket and spread it out a few feet from the flowers.

While they ate, Thelma told them more about Live Forevers.

"It's a real old fashioned plant; old fashioned even to my Mama. It takes over everything. Grass won't grow around it because it's so thick. It doesn't give in. That's why they've been around for centuries. And – " Thelma put down her ham sandwich and walked over to the nearest leaf. She plucked it from the stem and squeezed its milk out – "you can do this."

As the boys watched, she wiped the tip of the leaf and slowly blew into it. The leaf expanded outward, its veins arching. She pulled it away from her mouth and held it up at its tip, trapping her breath inside. She passed the small, oblong balloon in front of first Raynard, then Jesse and William's stilled faces.

"Plus," she continued, "you can make a whole new plant with one leaf."

The boys began to chew again, but glanced every now and then at the flowers.

Back on the road, Raynard played with the leaf he'd picked before they left. Occasionally he stole glances at his mother's hands on the steering wheel. In the back, Jesse teased William about Eileen, plucking at the shirt the girl brought William two nights before.

"I think she wants to marry you, Billy," Jesse said in a pseudoserious baritone. "Yeah she's fixin' on being a Woods. Already picking out your clothes."

William examined his brother cooly from across the seat, eyes almost shut from squinting so hard.

"You really need a psych scan, you know that?" William said. He shook his head sadly and looked out the window. Jesse kept up his banter.

Thelma smiled into the rearview mirror at them. It was true the Johnson girl came around a lot, but to Thelma, their quiet conversations seemed more companionable than romantic. Jesse was the son she'd have to worry about when it came to girls. Whatever they'd done to the hormones seemed to have a different effect on her youngest. William and Raynard got bigger; Jesse got hornier. She laughed to herself – wicked, but true. This only made his running diatribe funnier. She and Raynard exchanged a knowing glance.

"I'm just saying, Billy. Mrs. William Woods and you ain't even thirteen! That's a waste, man. Total loss."

"And just what is that supposed to mean, Jessup?" Thelma asked. Her relaxed shoulders belied the sharp tone.

William smiled and turned to Jesse.

"Yeah, Jessup, what's that supposed to mean?" he echoed.

Raynard put the leaf in his pocket and turned around in his chair, meaty hands hanging over the headrest. He cocked his head and joined the other two in staring Jesse down.

Under their combined gaze, Jesse smiled weakly, shifted his legs further across the aisle. Looking up to answer his mother, relief suddenly broke across his face. He pointed through the windshield.

"Is that it up there Mama?"

Thelma looked where he pointed. Thought to catch her breath, hummed instead.

"Most likely," she answered.

Thelma drove another quarter mile in the silent car. Pulled over into the grass.

Day had fully risen. Evergreen, maple brown and sky blue radiated from the landscape. In the branches of nearby maple trees, gray squirrels chased each other in

126

tight ellipses. Clouds of gnats swirled like dust in pockets of light. A honeysuckle scent, carried by the breeze, crossed the road, lingered and then changed direction.

All this was lost on the family sitting in the beat-up Verlanda that had carried them 500 miles from the inevitable to the birthplace of possibility.

The Woods sat silently, collecting their thoughts. They breathed as one. Thelma used her breath to clear her mind, so she could simply sit and witness. William got out first. He touched Jesse's shoulder, then slid out and waited by his mother's door, scanning the horizon.

As she took her first steps forward, her boys gathered around her.

The sight of what should have been Ezekiel Carter's boyhood home was as familiar to them as the path from Merigold to Mound Bayou. Someone had burned it, burned the house down, scorched the land. The trees even kept their distance. Ten paces lay between them and the hardy shrubs that tried to hide the shame. It had been years. That was obvious. How many Thelma couldn't tell. Fire had devastated the land around Mound Bayou since the boys were five; this seemed a bit older. Thelma stared at the open space – bare of marker, memorial, or explanation. She stared at it as she had stared at William's sullied clothes: her mind moving swiftly as the truth crept from the torrent of her thoughts. That day she had realized that the boys had done their own laundry for two years. Simply started after a patrol one day. By the time she heard the scrubbing, they already stood shirtless in their summer shorts hanging each garment carefully on the line outside. She'd looked at them from the back porch, smiling to herself in a plum sunset, thinking she had such sweet boys, such responsible boys.

Realization came quicker the second time around. She turned to Raynard, Jesse and sweet William, opened up her smile.

"We ought to get back on the road if we wanna get to Ms. Dullah's before supper. That's the softest bed between here and home," she tossed a look back at what they'd come for.

"Y'all ready?" she asked.

William looked at Jesse, Raynard at the edge of the parched earth, then at his brothers.

"Yes, Ma'am," Raynard answered.

Thelma pulled out her keys, swung them in a slow circle around her finger. The sun glinted on the ring, reflected it on her face.

"Ray, you go first. Then William. Then Jesse."

The boys looked at her quizzically.

"There's only thirty miles before we hit the highway. Let's make the most of it." Thelma sauntered towards the passenger side.

Comprehension dawned on Raynard's face and he grinned fit to split, expertly caught the key's Thelma tossed at him. Jesse opened the door for her with a broad sweep of his hand.

"Madame," Jesse sang.

"Thirty miles, Ray. That means you got ten minutes." William added from the backseat.

Thelma's scoff turned into a laugh.

"Billy, you got a sunstroke or something? Try twenty, maybe even forty minutes if y'all don't take this seriously."

Thelma sat back in her seat and carefully instructed Raynard on how to turn over the ignition. The Verlanda rumbled to life. Looking at Raynard, Thelma thought someone would have to grease their teeth to smile so big. Jesse and William grinned just as wide. As Raynard downshifted around a corner and the gears grinded their dissatisfaction, she worried for a second. But by the time Jesse rolled to a stop just before the on-ramp, she had to admit the boys took to it quick. Like they'd been born to do it.

Hell, MS

William rolled over in the rubble and breathed a heavy sigh. He no longer had the strength to scream. Instead, he stared up at the night sky, trying to look through the stars and out the other side of the universe. He was sure if he strained his eyes he would see his daughters there – and Lala, Raynard and Jesse, maybe even his mama if he looked deep enough. On the other side of the universe, they wouldn't be dead. He would still be lying in the rubble of Mound Bayou, bleeding a dark pool of pain into the ground beneath him, but that would be just fine, as long as his family was alive. William would stay here and stare for the rest of his life if it would un-explode the town, draw everyone's pieces back together and place Lala's hand in his.

When it happened, he'd been driving home from Merigold with the monthly supply of fresh water in the trunk. He always felt uneasy on the ride back. It unsettled him to be so near the new coast. He remembered when it had been land, before the Gulf of Mexico had swallowed up parts of Mississippi and Louisiana. He sat in the car with the residue of his uneasiness. A strange sensation settled into his spine and for a breath he couldn't breathe. He sealed the windows against the watery spirits of New Orleans. Though not superstitious, William respected what he didn't understand. He pressed down on the accelerator, hoping that their power would diminish the closer he got to home. Then the explosion. The blast was deafening. He fought to keep the car on the road as percussion pushed it sideways. Still, for what he found when he reached home, his soul needed more explanation than a loud noise in the dark.

The two massive oak trees that marked the entrance to Mound Bayou had disappeared. Only a toothy nest of roots jutted up from the ground. It sat in the middle of the road, blocking passage. William left the car parked in front of it. Upended, the roots were even taller than him. Staring out into the bright blaze that had been his hometown William grabbed onto one of the roots and squeezed it as he swallowed a quick jagged moan. Then he ran. Only later as he lay in the rubble of his home, would he remember what he saw as he moved: flames leaping up into the night, chewing up all the wood that hadn't been obliterated in the blast; lonely columns of concrete near the bank parking lot; the vault on its side 100 yards away; an arm sticking out of the gutter, on it a wedding ring reflecting the bright dazzle of flames.

After seeing that, William didn't expect to find Raynard or Jesse. He knew there was nothing left of his brothers if so little was left of the town.

There wasn't enough of William's neighborhood left to burn. The block was black and barren, quiet as a grave. When he reached it, the sudden darkness of it blinded William. He stumbled through it, afraid to slow down. Thirty meters away several bright lights hovered. Closer up he could see the lights were clearly fabric, white fabric stretched across crouched backs vulturing through the debris. Seven Klansmen laughed and drank in the middle of the ruined street.

William didn't think about it. He just killed them, used only his massive body and the controlled panic that flowed into his system when it was time to protect. The last of the white-cloaked men squeezed off a single singeing round that caught William in the back. A second later, that cloak bled red and the broken rifle settled next to the bodies of the other Klan.

If William had found Tash and Josephine beforehand, he would have made the men suffer. But as it was, he hadn't confirmed that his daughters were dead. So he killed quickly making sure he wouldn't be bothered while he searched.

He found the girls together, near the looking spot where Lala'd taught them about meteor showers and they wished on barely visible asteroid belts. Most of them was in one place.

He never found Lala. His wife had disappeared, just like the bank, the community center, and his neighborhood. They had all slipped away into nothingness.

And now here he lay, the something left behind. Moonlight spread across the Delta, reflected in pools and eddies of water that ebbed closer together every day, slowly but surely turning the Delta into an archipelago of stranded, hunted people. He had never accepted the ghost stories because this was his home, a home that he was proud to protect. But lying there, William knew Mississippi had finally become hell.

He heard faint footsteps coming closer. No doubt it was more of the Knight Klan. They would lynch William when they found him. Then Mound Bayou, after 235 years, would be no more.

A field mouse ran across his left foot and off into the woods, away from the smoke of the fallen town.

William's head pounded. For the first two days he hadn't noticed, but now his shock was well worn. And it became harder to believe he'd ever see through the stars or again into the hearts of the ones he loved. William listened to the men and their machines draw closer and closed his eyes.

A few feet away, near the bank of white and yellow flowers Raynard had planted years ago, two mounds of freshly-turned earth arched over the ground. A large hole, half the size of a transvan gaped next to them. It was just deep enough to keep animals away – just wide enough to accommodate William's broad shoulders.

William wouldn't yet get into the hole.

A sharp pain shot down his leg from his lower back, no doubt, the wound rubbing against one of the chunks of duocrete that used to be someone's house. William's fingers twitched in recognition, but the rest of him lay motionless, waiting.

He would kill the Klan coming to him and then climb into the hole.

He turned to it, drawing focus from its dark depths. The sides of his throat smacked together, spasming for moisture. Last night it had rained fat drops that pooled in pockets around him. He stuck his hand into one of them and brought it to his mouth, letting the dirty water slide down his throat.

William could hear voices now, still far off, but audible beneath the swell of cicadas. Judging from the change in volume over time, they would arrive in the next twenty minutes.

He rested his eyes on the sky and slowly stretched his toes inside his work boots. When he could feel circulation returning, he moved on to his ankles, and then his calves. He ran the blade in his left hand down a duocrete chunk, sharpening its jagged edge.

Up in a nearby sycamore, a splash of red caught his gaze, but a gust of wind carried it away before William could identify it. The wind pushed branches together and dislodged a chunk of wood trapped in the higher reaches.

It landed next to William with a loud thunk. A piece of the town's historical marker now lay next to his head. "887-" it read.

He heard feet shuffle through the underbrush not twenty meters from where he lay. Bright beams of ivory light broke up the darkness.

"Jake! Where you at, boy?" The voice had a touch of liquor in its Mississippi mud.

William had piled Jake and the rest of the Knight Klan bodies on the other side of town after he buried his children under the Live Forevers.

A second set of footsteps moved up from behind, this one accompanied by the bright orange pinpoint of a tracking scope. If they turned on the heat detection, William's ruse would be found out. He doubted that they would; they were in a ghost town.

He waited for the rest of the group to speak or move so he could track them. Without Raynard and Jesse, the process challenged his dulled, dehydrated senses, but in the next few minutes, William had a full count in his head; the plan of attack bypassed his brain and went straight to the muscles that would enact it. He looked up into the Seven Sisters, Tash's favorite constellation. The central star opened up in a flash of scintillation, shimmered blue, yellow, and white. And then William moved.

•

As the morning mist slicked the grass with ash, William Woods sat on the edge of his own grave and patted the earth that held his children. Staring across the clearing that had been his hometown, his mind superimposed the memory of its neat grid of streets and the people who had walked them.

He loved it all too much to get in the hole. In his place, he laid one handful of flowers inside. He stuffed another handful into his pocket and took a step out into the world. With him, went Mound Bayou.

An Open Letter to Your Readership

First an admission: The problem with being adaptable is there's nothing I can't do without.

I can hurt, hurt like hell, but I'll heal. I can be shattered and then have to find a way to drag my bag of bones down the road until the healing begins.

Sometimes it seems to never end: the pain, the tears, the scab, the itch, the ache. The scars.

Even when the pain is unbearable it will be born. I, for instance, lost everyone in an instant. My children, wife and brothers, nearly every person I had ever known: destroyed. The Knight Klan's bombs left them in pieces and me to witness it.

And what did I do after I saw what was left of everyone I loved, after I smelled them burning and found myself the only person left alive in the smoldering wilderness?

I healed.

I thought then that my body had betrayed me. Now I know that though the missing pieces may make me smaller when I come back together, in a fashion, I am whole.

You should know this because soon some of you will be like me – not quite a Carter Kid, but something more. You will one day be 67 and look 32; Years will pass and you will feel as if you've aged a single day.

In 72 hours, you should have all the proof you need. But I'm an impatient man, even at my age, so I'll tell you now if you've the mind to hear it. Or come back to this in three days. We still have choices, more than we had before really – or soon enough we will.

Remember this: If it's only the body that heals, a person goes mad. I did. I had my decade of delirium and depression when I melted away. During that time, I did only one thing deliberately: I went north, away from the water.

My youngest daughter used to say she could hear spirits whispering to her in the babble of water, in its brooks, creeks, and bayous. But she was brave, my girl. She'd grab my hand and whisper right back to it. On the way home, she'd tell me what the water had said.

After I lost her, there were things I didn't want to hear.

In time the truth became deafening. This condition can do that – but it's only wisdom. I used to believe you could love someone so much that without that person, your heart would stop in protest. I believed that it should. I liked believing that; it made the world worth the struggle to stay in it. But now I know that something in me insists on living. And to be honest, I don't know if it's the genetic advantages, a curse, or some part of me I can't call a friend.

But I've decided it's a good thing. 'Cause it's better to see things with your own eyes – even hard things, even the worst things. I know because I've seen some of them and missed others, and it's the ones I missed that I regret.

Most people only know what's in the world by what they're told. They have to take someone's word for it, though they don't think of it that way. It's the limitation of memory: it has a beginning, and if it started too late, it started too late. The net has saved us from the old limits of distance. With access, anyone can link into a camera or eavesdrop on a conversation thousands of miles away, but for all that ingenuity, we still can't bend time and go into the past to see what happened before. Still, the past changes. People change it all the time. But a lot of folks would never believe that unless they could see it in their own lives.

For example, did you know the former national recreation area Land Between the Lakes wasn't sold to a private fishery as it was reported thirty years ago? I've been there and there's no fishery; there never was. There was however a small collection of families living there once – in the lakes between the land. They had barrel chests and deep, murky voices like they all had the worst colds you ever heard. They slept underwater, in clumps, to protect themselves and each other, but they're gone from there now. Innovation Tech I think it was that rounded them up. I wasn't there that particular night, but IT genetic registry officers had been in the area. Any more than that I can't say for sure because I didn't see it myself.

I know you don't believe me. You don't have to. It doesn't make it any less true.

History is written by the victors, they say. That's because enough of them survive to be dominant, and to write their story. So here we find ourselves: Me writing, and you reading your morning news in a moment that stands outside time, a historical moment.

Because I've decided to share. I've decided the have-nots should have something.

When I was a kid, people used to say, 'as long as I have my health'. Then they stopped, because the wealthy took it for granted and everyone else knew if they ever were lucky enough to have good health, it would one day disappear, sapped by the places they lived and the death that would come creeping or crashing into their lives.

Dr. Carter began to change that and the rich didn't shine as they once had. Not everything about their life was better. Some of you can't imagine how that felt: that something the wealthy had was not inherently better. I've yet to come across anything more transformative.

But I can't offer what Dr. Carter did. And I'm not offering it to all of you.

This morning I sent my DNA samples, you can call them MoBay, to five labs. But I did my research. Those labs do not include any private corporations, subsidiaries, or feeder clinics. They serve only at-risk people in financial need. In other words, the DNA is not currently for sale. That is not its purpose right now. If the future owners should decide to offer it for trade that is their business. If we must get our equality by trading life for power then so be it.

The samples are contained in self-degrading cultures, suitable only for quick diagnostics, just enough to prove not who I am but how I am. Any attempt to do otherwise will hasten their decomposition.

From what I've seen the world is about to change more than any of us can anticipate.

And after all these years, I've learned that hope is the one thing I won't do without any longer. But I want hope for us all.

Here is where we begin.

ABOUT THE AUTHOR

After time well spent in alphabet cities – NYC, ATL, and DC – Tenea D. Johnson lives near the beach under a 300-year-old oak where she writes speculative fiction and makes music. Her short fiction and poetry have appeared in various magazines and anthologies. A poetry collection *Starting Friction* was published in 2008 (Mayapple Press). Her audio work will soon be available through counterpoise records, where great stories breed with great music to spawn superior entertainment. Her debut novel *Smoketown* (Blind Eye Books) was published earlier this year.

Made in the USA
Charleston, SC
11 November 2011